THE SINGING FOREST

H. MORTIMER BATTEN

❀ ❀ ❀

THE
SINGING
FOREST

Illustrated by Maurice Wilson

NEW YORK / FARRAR, STRAUS AND COMPANY

AUTHOR'S NOTE

This book is the result of forty years in the deer forests of the Scottish Highlands, stalking every summer and hind shooting or working the hill cairns for foxes in winter. Practically every incident in the life of Corrie is true. The story of his days as the pet of the laird's children is based on that of a red deer calf my children reared at Killin. He was blessed by the old Highland woman when the children were blessed, and he grew up to be a Royal.

H. M. B.

GLOSSARY

BRACKEN: any tall coarse fern.

BRAE: a hillside; a slope.

CLACHAN: a hamlet; a cluster of houses.

CORRIE: a circular hollow in the side of a mountain—often with steep sides.

HARBOR: the sheltering place of a deer.

HIND: the female deer.

KNOBBER: a two-year-old stag.

LAIRD: a landowner, usually of several thousand acres. He is not necessarily a lord, or member of the peerage.

LOCH: a lake; also, a nearly landlocked bay.

ROYAL: a mature stag with at least twelve points on his antlers.

SASSENACH: an Englishman; also a Scottish landowner.

SCREE: a jumble of rocks, often at the base of a cliff.

STRATH: a flat river valley; bottom lands.

TARN: a steep-banked lake or pool.

TINKER: a gypsy; a vagrant.

THE SINGING FOREST

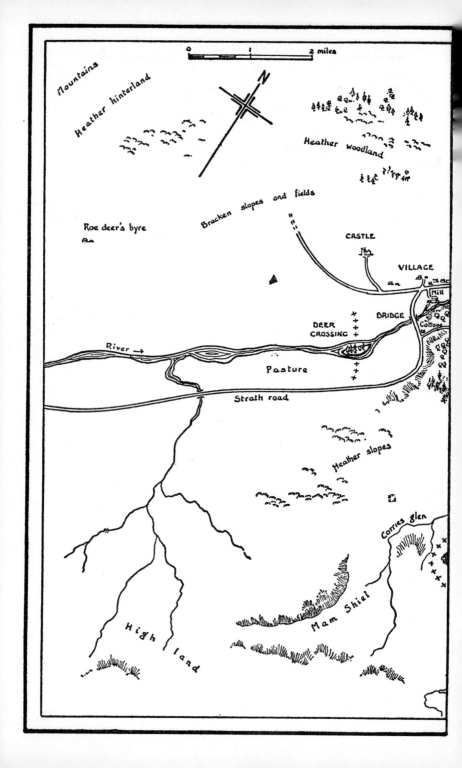

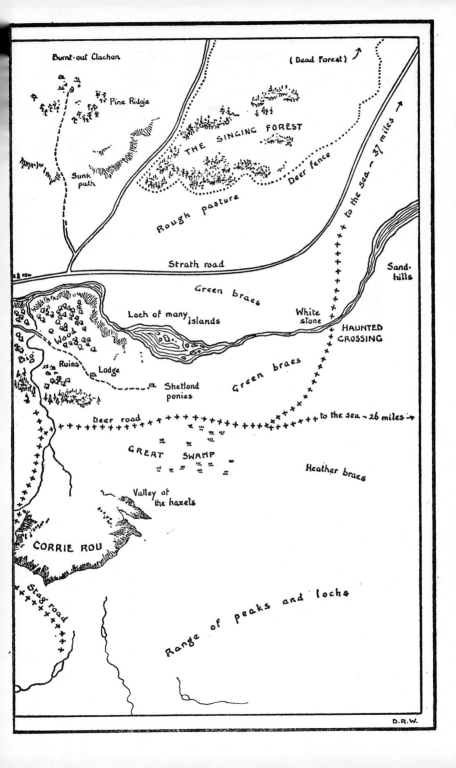

CHAPTER 1

The laird and his gamekeeper lay at the edge of the great peat swamp below the heights of Corrie Rou. The sun was setting behind the barrier of mountains, so that the light was in their eyes, and they were looking at a wall of blackness through what might have been a gigantic gossamer curtain, the skyline pin-pointed sharp against the last light of the June day. On all sides the peat pools shone like crimson mirrors, till in the shadows the farthest glimmered gold. Over the swamp itself it was dark, except where the higher ridges caught the sunbeams and every sprig of heather shone like a spray of jewels. The effect was weird, almost unearthly, and strangest of all was the silence, for there was activity on all sides. Activity and movement, but no sound.

They were there to take stock of the deer herds, and the level swamp was full of deer. A fair number of hinds, as female deer are called, already had their new calves running with them, for the deer of the Corrie Rou habitually descend to the swamp to graze at the day's closing. Tonight, as MacEwen the gamekeeper had prophesied, the weather had brought down more deer than usual, but though the swamp was creeping with them, only a few were visible at any given moment. Now and then a herd of knobbers would suddenly rise and remain a few moments in sharp relief, then they would dip into the shadows again. The horns of all the stags were in the velvet. Sometimes a tenpointer or a twelve-pointer would rise up, but at least eighty per cent were hinds, young hinds and old, for this was hind country.

Had the light been normal, something like two hundred deer might have been visible, for tonight they were all down from the Forestry Commission plantings and the corries and washouts, from the screes and the ptarmigan hinterlands and the wide plateaus of Corrie Rou, which is the focal point of the whole vast deer forest, the central feature from which the whole area takes its name.

The deer were there to feed and for no other purpose, and though some of them drifted in herds, not one of them seemed conscious of its neighbors. Not a grunt or a bark or the shrill whistle of a nervous hind broke the quietude of the terrace. Moreover, there was no scent, or if there was the deer chose to ignore it, for there is no telling how they will react to prevailing conditions. Had the two men lying side by side in the old heather raised a rifle and shot the beast nearest to them, it is more than likely that there would have been no response at all from the others, so the laird hardly troubled to lower his voice. "Look at that young fellow, Ewen, following the big grey-faced stag!" he exclaimed. "He can't be many days old. Why isn't he following his mother instead of that braw beast?"

The two deer were not a hundred yards away. The stag was probably a Royal, and at his heels, following his every movement, ran a dappled calf of that season—clearly a little stag, for they are quite differently shaped from the hind calves. The little creature might have been the big stag's shadow, so closely he followed, and the old grey-face, the finest strain of the Corrie Rou, would have tipped the beam at well over 300 pounds. He had certainly attained his prime and more than likely was past it.

"Ye ken, sir, as well as I do, that a stag calf will often follow a big stag," replied Ewen Mac-Ewen a shade impatiently. "They're the same as the other wee menfolk—like to be with the men as soon as they can toddle. I'm thinking his mother will no be far away."

As he spoke the two deer stood against the light, no more than silhouettes; then suddenly the big stag flung round, so that in a moment they were face to face, their shadows falling darkly across the ridge. The men expected the big beast to thrust the calf aside, for as a rule old stags are intolerant of the very young, and had it been a hind calf that undoubtedly would have happened; but now they were to see one of the prettiest incidents imaginable.

Finding himself under the nose of his hero, the calf lifted his face much as a child might have done to be kissed. The gesture was exactly that, and the king stag responded. Lowering his great head he licked the little fellow's face and ears in the most caressing manner possible.

"That's pretty, Ewen—never saw anything prettier," muttered the laird. "I'll wager it's his own calf!—nothing on this earth more clearly proven!"

"Of course it's ain calf," said Ewen. "They aye ken their ain."

The laird sought the face of his old servant. "It surely takes a wise father to know his own in the deer forests," he observed. "Think of all the calves in Corrie Rou, so how in the world do you tell me——?"

"By their scent, of course," replied Ewen. "Sir, I've seen it more times than I can remember. How does a vixen fox ken her ain cubs—or a bitch her ain puppies—aye, even though you mix them with twenty other pups in the kennels?"

The conversation was interrupted by the appearance of a sorely crippled hind between them and the two deer. Slowly, painfully, she mounted the ridge, all hunched up and half dragging her hindquarters as though her spine had been broken.

"Heaven have mercy on us!" exclaimed the laird. "She's no ornament to the forest whatever! What in wonderment do you want leaving a poor cripple like that—littering up the ground?"

"Rheumatics!" retorted Ewen, then added more gently, "now hold your remarks, sir, while I'm telling ye. That hind is as well able to look after herself and her calf as any other hind whatever. Whiles she's badly, whiles she's better. She's as fat as butter."

"Rheumatism!" echoed the laird incredulously. "She's a disabled and suffering beast and no one wants to see the likes of her hobbling over the braes."

"She's been hobbling ower the braes the last five years," stormed Ewen. "She throws a good stag calf every other year, and that calf over there with the big stag is as like as not hers. We'll soon see."

The two had known each other all their lives, stalked together, shot together, fished and soldiered together, and such tiffs were the normal routine.

The laird waved savagely as though to dismiss the subject, but Ewen was not to be so lightly put off his ground. He knew every deer on the home braes and was sensitive to criticism of any one of them. They were his children.

Ewen growled. "She never was shot at!" he reiterated. "I saw what happened with my ain calf eight—maybe nine—autumns ago. She got underfoot of one of thae big yellow-faced stags. Three times he ran the calf out, then when she came back the fourth time he threw her five or six yards. She lay on her back and I thought she was dead, though when I went up she was off like the wind. She's been lame ever since, although she's worse at times than others—Now watch for yourself—look ye! What have I telt ye?"

For a fresh move had started among the deer. Both men had been conscious of the faintest movement of air coming from behind them, and in a few seconds up went the heads of every stag and hind in view. Those on the ridges at once began to drain into the hollows, those in the hollows rose to the ridges. All were streaming away at the edges of the great swamp, but without haste or particular concern—all but the crippled hind nearest to them. She was looking straight at her calf, which was running towards her and a few seconds later stood glued to his mother's side—the calf which had been following the big stag.

"Well, she threw a good one there," the laird admitted. "What's disturbing them, Ewen?"

Ewen searched the skies, suspicious of the presence of His Majesty, but there was no eagle in view. "Scented us," he answered, but as he spoke they saw the crippled hind bound aside, and with an agility that surprised them she struck with her fore-hoofs into a clump of old heather alongside the calf. At the same instant a fox leaped out of the clump. He was one of the biggest mountain foxes they had ever seen, more like a wolf than the little red foxes of the long valley. His white fangs were bared and his face distorted in a vulpine leer at being so roughly roused by the hind, and as he bounded off the stag calf was straight in his way. With a whisk of his long brush and a steely click of jaws Reynard hustled the little animal aside, bowling him clean over; then he vanished into the hollows as only a fox can.

Both men rose, and behind them appeared a third member of the party hitherto unseen as he lay obediently flattened in the deep heather. It was Don, MacEwen's deerhound, who knew as much about the deer of that forest as Ewen himself. Part deerhound he was, part Labrador, a mighty dog with the strength of a mastiff.

Don, low in the heather, had not seen the fox, and the fox scent had escaped him as it had escaped the hind till the moment she struck. When the dog rose he saw only the stricken hind, and Don had been trained to single out wounded deer and either bay them or pull them down. So, when Ewen clicked his fingers, the mistake was pardonable—Don bounded straight towards the hind.

"Och!" cried Ewen. "Nothing will stop him now!"

The hind looked up, and when she saw that vision of death bounding towards her she simply shuddered and froze to the ground, and next moment Don appeared to throw her clean over his shoulder.

The calf was running round in circles bleating pitiably, while MacEwen took the long-bladed knife from his belt and approached the dying hind. "Och!" he repeated. "A pity Don did not see that fox."

There was no going back on it now—the stag calf had lost his mother. "I never saw a fox more vicious," observed the laird. "If it's a vixen, Ewen, she may have cubs in the heather."

Ewen shook his head. "It was a dog-fox, sir," he stated. "Look what he's done to that calf's ear! Split it half-way down from the tip."

The laird nodded. "We don't need to ear-mark him anyway," said he. "By that sign we shall know him all the days of his life."

Ewen nodded towards the stag calf, who stood sniffing his poor dead mother. "What about him?" he asked. "He's a greyface, best blood on the range, and I'm thinking the fox will be back for him if we leave him here."

"We'll take him home," replied the laird. "He'll make a nice pet for the children."

Evidently the calf was younger than they had thought, for having yielded to the little animal's desire to suck his fingers the laird had no difficulty in laying hands on him. He carried him over, but in spite of the calf's extreme infancy his strength was surprising, and he was the most awkward little bundle imaginable. He seemed all corners and elbows. "Certainly no need to ear-mark him," he confirmed.

Ewen quickly tied the calf's four legs and placed him over his shoulders.

"Now back to our horses," said the laird. "You'll need to return with a spade tomorrow, Ewen."

The sun was off the slopes, and the chills of the June evening were descending as they left the ill-fated swamp. The scents of spring, merging into the fuller scents of summer, were astir across the forest, from the peat swamp and the pine woods and the primrose braes by the river, touched by the faint tang of balsam from foresters' fires in the plantings. As Ewen mounted his pony and re-adjusted his living load he remarked, "The crippled hind no hae a chance, poor thing."

❧ ❧ ❧

CHAPTER 2

It is generally true that no greater misfortune can come to a wild animal than that it should fall into man's heedless care and keeping; but the stag calf Corrie—Corrie of Corrie Rou, as he was spontaneously named—was fortunate. In the first place, captivity is not the same cruel break for a grazing animal as it is for one of predatory habits; in the second, Corrie went to an ideal home.

It is unlikely that Corrie would have survived had not the laird taken him home that night, and under the unnatural conditions which became his lot he at least survived his tenderest days well sheltered from hunger and danger. Even fear itself he hardly knew till he reached adolescent understanding, while he had playmates to fill the unnatural gap, and certainly an abundance of reciprocal affection.

On their arrival at the castle Corrie was handed over to the laird's two children, and Callum, old MacEwen's son, who acted as general factotum about the place, was called in as adviser.

Callum was a grave young man in his early twenties, sprung from a line that had served the family as gamekeepers for generations. His knowledge of nature was profound, his love of and loyalty to the laird and the children a matter of inheritance. His judgment stood unchallenged in all matters affecting their pets; he was their adviser and guardian in most things concerning the gentler phases of their home life. At one time a goodly number of deer calves were fed on the estate, and to Callum in his early youth had fallen the task of rearing them. Therefore, no better adviser could have existed for Corrie's "wet nurse" days.

When the laird suggested fresh milk watered down Callum's disapproval was absolute. "Do you know, sir, cow's milk is the thinnest milk on earth except human milk?" said he. "What any wild animal requires is a little and often, and that little good and strong. Goat's milk is better, but even that should be thickened up by the white of an egg and a little chalk. Best of all is the powdered milk for babies, and that mixed double strength. Give him that for a week and he'll never look ahint him, and after that we can think of cow's milk with maybe a wee bit of gruel. Give him weak food now and it will just be a matter of rickets and a sickly calf."

The laird's plan to house Corrie in the old summerhouse by the putting green was similarly turned down. "Mind, sir, I'm not against the idea altogether," replied the young Highlandman, "but for a week or longer he'll need constant attention. That will fall upon me and Miss Fiona and Master Alastaire, and the children won't want tramping across the wet grass late every evening and early morning. He'll be a clean wee beastie; far better to give him a basket in the nursery for a while— if madam will not object."

"Good heavens!" exclaimed the laird. "What we have let ourselves in for! He'd better have a nursery and a day and night nurse to himself!"

"Well, sir, I'm telling ye," pursued Callum remorselessly. "It's only for a few days, and after that he'll be no more trouble. Meantime he'll need his hot milk every three hours, last feed at bedtime and first at daybreak. Or else he'll just fall sick and sleep his life away. A young wild animal has very little hold on life, and without their mothers they just slip between your fingers the moment they're sick."

The laird's children were Fiona, aged ten, and Alastaire, due for boarding school next year. The baby, still in her cot, hardly entered the picture. On one side of the big day-nursery a circular basket was filled with heather for Corrie. Two other frequent occupants of this happy room were to prove personalities of no small standing in Corrie's life— Chang, the Pekingese, and old Bongo, the golden Labrador whom everybody loved. (Don, Mac-Ewen's deerhound, was not a member of the family circle.) No sooner had Corrie drunk his first bottle of milk from Fiona's gentle hands than the fun started. Chang, who last week had worried a bantam and killed and eaten Fiona's guinea pig, made it plain that he resented this trespass of an unknown wildling upon their innermost sanctuary. He indicated that Corrie would meet the same fate as the contemptible guinea pig if the matter were left to him, whereupon Bongo, with his higher understanding, planted himself stolidly between Corrie and Chang, and forthwith appointed himself responsible for their new pet's safety. Not till

Chang had been damped down under several cushions did the snarling and barking cease, then Corrie, in his mottled coat and revived by the warm food, took spirited possession of the floor. Within twenty minutes he and Chang were sending the mats flying in all directions on the polished floor, and so began a partnership whose strength must stand as almost unique between two animals so far apart in character and breeding.

In every incident of Corrie's first days one saw the pattern of the wild deer, the same sudden promptings, the same instincts, the same natural fears, and this became more and more so as he grew older. From that first bottle he never looked behind him, and certainly there was not the least indication of his falling into the torpor of sickness Callum had described as so dangerous. From that time on, his life became one of almost unbroken laughter-provoking merriment.

The calf quickly learned his feeding times, which Fiona was most meticulous in observing. Almost on the minute his hunger bleat would ring through the house, a cry more high-pitched than that of a lamb or goat kid—a brief stab of sound intended to penetrate storm and distance. It was unmistakably a wild-animal cry, and assuredly it would have reached the keen ears of his mother over a great distance. At that time of the year the hinds do not stand over their calves as they lie obediently in their trampled beds in the heather or bracken, for in that way they would merely advertise the whereabouts of their young. The hind goes right away to some higher point from which she can watch the place where the calf is hidden, and since they have their recognized nursery territories, the cry of a single calf in peril will bring all the mothers of the neighborhood stampeding defensively to the place. There was only this difference—that Corrie in his sheltered life, with no eagle overhead and no grey fox prowling the hollows, would cry out at the least provocation, whereas a wild calf never cries till it actually sees its mother approaching, or has other good cause. Then up it gets, with that shrill bleat, and in a second or two a dozen calves all round are up and bleating, and a dozen anxious mothers stepping up to silence them. Should the cry be one of anguish when no mother is near, then be sure the mothers will be pounding in from all quarters to annihilate the enemy or to drive it off, and thus one sees the value of the communal nurseries.

Corrie soon outgrew the nursery stage, and began to show his eagerness for extended freedom. Whenever the nursery door was opened he would make a dash for it, frequently to the consternation of the nurse with her tray of baby requirements. Thus it became customary for anyone wishing to enter the room to knock respectfully, whereupon those already there would fall upon Corrie and hold him pinioned till the door was safely closed again.

"Let him out—let him out," advised the laird. "Make him a bed in the summerhouse. No sense in keeping a red deer calf cooped up indoors."

So Callum penned off a corner of the old summerhouse and made a deep bed for him, and when he had established that as his home, Corrie showed his independence by using the window as a way of entrance and exit in preference to the door: if the door were left open he would immediately nose it shut. His next step was to proclaim the surrounding putting green as undividedly his personal property, on which only a favored few were permitted to trespass. Not even Chang was included, no one, indeed, but the two children and Callum. Other members of the household were immediately pushed and prodded till they moved off, this being one of the first of the little stag characteristics to exert itself. The putting green was his domain, and he the king stag who marshals his hinds and will admit of no intruders.

Thus a more independent phase of Corrie's life began, and quickly he responded to his freedom. Fiona's devotion and gentleness made up in his life what it lacked by his unnatural bereavement, for she was an attractive and winning little girl, and he was always restless without her. Then came rather a wide gap in the young deer's affections, till somewhat casually they embraced Alastaire, Callum and Chang, while Bongo he regarded as grandfather of his little clan, there mainly to be sought for protection, but always to be treated respectfully.

Alastaire did not approve of the blue ribbon his sister was wont to tie about her pet's neck—a blue ribbon with an absurd little silver bell that tinkled when he ran. He would point at it and laugh, and of all human sounds Corrie disliked laughter most. A little mockery of this kind and he would put down his head and push Alastaire this way and that till Fiona intervened.

"Why don't you get him a proper leather collar

2 4

instead of making a sissy of him?" Alastaire said; and indeed it soon became evident that something of the kind to protect Corrie's throat would be advisable, and this on account of Chang's many disreputable friends among the village dogs. In spite of all his superior airs and self-importance, Chang was anything but a snob where his personal friends were concerned, and many and varied was the canine assortment he invited to scamper over the laird's grounds. Many had sprung from the furious little cairn terriers used in the ceaseless warfare against the hill foxes, and these would not have been averse to worrying a young wild animal that was clearly out of place. So the red collar, complete with brass points, was bought, at first so slack that there was no need to unbuckle it to slip it over his head, and one more step towards the departure of Corrie's babyhood was achieved.

Yet his hold upon life was evidently not so robust as his strength and vitality led one to believe; for at about this time the children were bidden to visit friends in Edinburgh, and Corrie was left to Callum's keeping—a responsibility the grave-faced young man did not accept very cheerfully.

That day the calf searched for Fiona in the

garden long and ceaselessly, running hither and thither with his piercing bleat at every fresh sound. By evening his hopes began to languish, and he refused his bottle. He would not even accept treacle gingerbread, but merely wrinkled up his little moist nose when it was offered to him. Next morning he again refused his bottle and continued his search: at midday Callum found him still unresponsive, and his nose was no longer moist. Callum shook his head gravely. That evening Corrie went to the door of the nursery and lay down beside it. Still he refused his bottle and his eyes had begun to lose their sparkle, so Callum did the only thing he could do. He found an old garment belonging to Fiona and spread it out by the nursery door for Corrie to lie upon. He knew that Corrie would not leave that place till his mistress returned, for to his mind Fiona rightly belonged to that corner of the house.

Then Callum sought the girl's mother and told her. "I'm sorry, madam," said he, "but Corrie is simply pining. Unless Miss Fiona returns very soon she will find no pet awaiting her."

"That must not happen, Callum," replied the mistress of the house. "How long is this going to last? I do not wish to appear heartless, but it will be rather inconvenient if the child can never go away."

"Only another week or so, madam," Callum assured her. "We must realize the calf is only a fortnight old. Give him another week and it will be safe to leave him."

His mistress nodded. "All right," she answered, "I will telephone Edinburgh now. You can take it that I'll want you to meet the children on the early afternoon train tomorrow."

But by morning poor Corrie was very far through, and only Callum's understanding hand kept the smoldering fire burning. Sips of weak brandy, milk and treacle were no more than holding the enemy from the door, and it was the laird—quite the world's worst driver—who eventually took the car to the station with Ewen at his side to advise, so that the journey must have been a lively running commentary.

Callum remained on duty, and it seemed to him that the car would never return. He knew that the calf's life was slipping between his fingers, and he took Corrie in his arms, hanging on to him as though clinging to life itself—just a little longer, a little longer! He talked to him, carried him to the window, exercised his limbs, showed him

Chang and Bongo, did everything he could to re-kindle some spark of interest, but the long ears drooped, the square little head sank, and into Callum's heart came a sense of defeat at having failed both the animal and its little mistress.

Then there sounded the closing of a heavy door, and a shrill voice cried, "Corrie! Corrie! Where is he, mother?"

Callum threw open the nursery door. "Here, Miss Fiona!" he cried. "I have him in my arms. Come quickly."

That evening Corrie drank four bottles of milk and still bleated for more. His independence of the nursery returned and he romped back to the summerhouse. Callum went off to the sawmill across the road grinning from ear to ear between intervals of whistling, for though it had been but an incident in a man's life he was conscious of a great and single-handed achievement.

Under any circumstances little wild animals are difficult to rear, for they have no fear of death in its less violent forms. Death by blood and violence they understand, but there is always the danger of their falling into that torpor of sickness from which there is no rousing them. Once they lose interest in life they allow it to slip away without any attempt to hold it, a characteristic that belongs strongly to the red deer. But after that day Corrie throve apace both in mind and body, and his mental advance was shown from day to day by his growing sense of ownership.

Not only Chang, but Chang's village friends soon learned that the putting green was solely Corrie's. It was brought home to them by the sharpness of Corrie's fore-hoofs and the strength of his punch, and the complaining "kia-aw-aw" of a stricken cur making for the garden hedge was soon a familiar sound. So Chang's friends ceased to visit the castle garden, and as for cats——!

Corrie's hoof-marks on the flower-beds were mere pinpricks, but many pinpricks soon make a beaten path, and ere long the garden was a veritable maze of beaten paths, a miniature of the great forest from which he had come, where the deer trails checkered the whole range leading to and from their appointed feeding and sheltering places. Always, like his wild kindred, he came and went by the same ways; these paths were individually his own, interconnecting the various points he visited daily. One day the laird said to his gardener, "Far too many dogs using this place,

MacDiarmid. You'll have to put up some wire-netting to keep them out."

"Dogs!" echoed MacDiarmid. "Those aren't dog paths, they're deer paths! He must have ten miles of them about these grounds, and from his way of living it's just the same as the deer forest. There's no checking him."

There was a wild-deer reasoning behind all of Corrie's comings and goings, and a perfectly clear explanation why he took so naturally to many of the children's games, but could never be made to play an understanding part in others. Children's games are but imaginative elaborations of the games little wild animals have played for ages past. He naturally mastered hide-and-seek so far as the seeking was concerned, but he could never grasp the hiding part of the business, since there was no eagle in the skies and no scent of fox in the air. He was glad enough to remain hidden so long as the pressure of his mistress's hand was on his head, but immediately that pressure was relaxed Corrie —like Chang—considered the uninteresting scene ended. But when it came to the seeking, Corrie knew that one or more of his beloved band of play-mates was missing, and he would not rest till they were restored to the party. There was no hiding from Corrie, for that little wet nose of his was a quick and certain finder.

Generally, at the most crucial moments, Chang would discover a real or imaginary cat lurking in the camp, and away he would go with flying ears and whisking tail, Corrie hard behind him. For Corrie hated cats with a real and bitter hatred, and if he found the cat scent on one of his private deer paths, he would spend the next ten minutes beating out the shrubs and snorting through the thickets.

Just so far did his wild instincts extend, and no further. How often, when red calves are playing together, will one of them suddenly seem to become instinctively frightened in the heat of the game, and clap down as though terror-stricken behind a rock. There it will remain, ears down, head down, flat as a rug, till presently its play-mates realize that one is missing, and joyously scamper back to paw it from its couch. But it is instinctive fear that bids that calf clap down, a faint scent, or the sight of a buzzard in the sky, and Corrie was yet without that incentive.

The world-old game of King of the Castle he loved and understood. Therein some high point had to be held or stormed, and not five miles away one would have seen the wild deer calves, many of them together, playing the same game in the soft evening twilight—one of them boldly holding some rocky pinnacle, while the others sought to dispose of him and take the point of eminence themselves.

The "herd games" Corrie thoroughly understood—namely, those breathless moments when between games the party herded together before moving to some fresh ploy. Then, particularly where the way narrowed, he would crowd close to his mistress, his delicate nostrils quivering, his eyes on the skies, and, though it was all pretense, it was evident from a hundred signs a day that he was the little wild animal at heart, and that civilization was but a veneer. One versed in the ways of the wild deer could see always that Corrie, though one of the party, was playing the game on his own, the game of his own people in their mountain surroundings.

That his wild instincts were there and never relaxed was shown by his attitude towards the eagle. Every fourth day, as regular as the clock, one of the pair which nested on the great cliffs of the Corrie Rou would circle high over the house, systematically working the green braes of the valley. Buzzards circled there every day, often eight or nine of them together, and at any height it takes a practiced eye to discriminate between the buzzard and the eagle. Often the eagle passed over at an immense altitude, no more than a speck in the heavens, but Corrie always knew of its approach long before it was visible to human eyes. Up would go his head and up would go his ears. For a minute or so he would stand absolutely still, then he would melt away to one particular corner, where an old ruined wall ran out forming a corner with the wall of the barn. As he stood close against the wall he might have known that he exactly matched it in color, and there he would remain till the eagle finally vanished over the skyline.

"Och, sir, he kens, you understand, he kens!" said Callum to the laird. "Many hold that the eagle is not of much consequence to the red deer, but, believe me, the eagle, when in the mood, is a very dangerous enemy. He will strike at near anything that moves, particularly when the clouds are low down on the hill."

Though virtually the fool of the party and an eternal source of laughter, Chang was brave. His teeth were so loose that far from being the mighty hunter he imagined himself, he could not have held a rabbit even if he caught one. One memorable day, indeed, a baby bunny ran straight into his open mouth, and though Chang chewed it for a full minute it eventually got up and ran away unhurt. He would now join with Corrie in chasing any of his old friends out of the garden, and the bigger the dog the more furiously would Chang attack it. But he had one all-pervading fear—he was gun-shy. Anything in the way of an explosion he could not tolerate. If he saw a child pick up a paper bag it was enough. Away he would run—into the linen cupboard, into the furnace room in the cellar, anyway, anywhere, lest the child should inflate the bag and burst it.

Corrie had no fear of such reports, but in time it was shown that he and Chang had one great fear in common—thunder. At the first rumble over the hills both of them would disappear, not to emerge till the storm was over. Where they went no one knew. One day the thunder was continuous, storm following storm. So long were the two absent that the children went out to search for them. They searched the greenhouses, the shrubberies and the hayloft, but there was neither news nor sign of the delinquents. Eventually the services of the ever faithful Callum were enlisted, and Callum took the matter by no means lightly. For Corrie he had no fears, but for Chang——! He had known gun-shy dogs to disappear completely during such storms. They had been seen running wildly into the distance, never to appear again. Whether they had fallen over cliffs or drowned themselves in the torrents no man was ever to know. Callum was anxious for Chang— the foolish little dog so much a member of the precious home circle.

Callum searched and returned dripping from brow to boot toe, but still shaking his head anxiously. He set out over the same ground again, and eventually he found them. They were deeply buried under Corrie's bed in the summerhouse, Chang snoring asthmatically at the bottom of the heap with Corrie spread out on top of him.

Corrie's infancy was slipping by with the lengthening of the summer days. He was becoming more and more headstrong, more and more disposed to overstep the narrow laws of convention to which our domestic animals submit naturally. Still pretty in his sun-flaked coat, as dainty a playmate as

any little lady could have, he began to take dis-
likings towards certain people. The telegraph-boy
teased him with a ginger biscuit, whereupon he
"took a scunner," not only at the boy himself, but
at anyone wearing a uniform. His head was now
hard; he was able to stand up on his hind legs
and strike out with his forelegs, and a blow across
the face would have left its mark.

It was Alastaire who first learned this, for the
son of the house sprang from a long line of soldier
ancestors, and he held that a young wild animal
which must inevitably return to its own place in
life should learn to guard its own interests. So he
would put on the boxing gloves and deal Corrie
a dab or two, and if Corrie refused to fight he
would very soon receive a light cuff on his split
ear, which always enraged him. Up he would rear
on his hind legs, whereafter Alastaire's part consisted in warding off the thrusts of Corrie's fore-
hoofs.

But one day the boy's defense failed, and he
had to go to his mother with a graze extending
from his brow to his mouth and blood dripping
from his chin. Of course he was full of excuses
for Corrie, who was in no way to blame. The fault

was entirely his own for having failed to ward off the blow he had deliberately invited.

"I quite understand," his mother agreed, "but in future you had better wear your fencing-mask for these engagements. Corrie is stronger now, and the fore-hoofs of deer are dangerous weapons."

The sight of Alastaire with half his face in plaster perhaps enhanced the admiration of the village boys, but it did not improve Corrie's position with their mothers. The boy might have lost an eye, and so might any of their small sons who went to the castle with messages. Did madam realize that the deer calf was no longer a safe playmate for children? What a pity it would be if he scarred the bonny face of Miss Fiona!—and quite clearly Corrie should now be returned to the hill.

Old MacDiarmid, who attended the flower-borders surrounding the house, held kindred views; for there was nothing Corrie loved better than to catch this valued old gardener bedding out his young plants. Then Corrie would approach silently and swiftly by one of his own beaten paths, and having delivered the matador's thrust would be gone before MacDiarmid could collect himself.

But one day the old man was just too quick for him and, turning, he hurled his trowel. The tool caught Corrie a clatter across his split ear, and the calf went down like a felled ox. "Oh, poor wee beastie! Poor wee beastie!" cried the old man in remorse, thinking he had slain Fiona's pet, but before he could reach the spot Corrie was up and bouncing away like a rubber ball, a creature completely demented. He leaped the wicket-gate with a foot to spare and MacDiarmid heard the rattle of his hoofs across the road. The gardener returned to his work, satisfied that he had taught the mischievous little varmint a lesson.

From the other side of the main road a narrow lane ran down to the riverside mill that cut the estate timber and supplied the house and the village with power. In an outbuilding of the old mill they kept the fishing rods, and having put his rod away Alastaire emerged into the lane. There he saw Corrie careering towards him, his ears laid back, his eyes shining, running as he had never run before. Alastaire saw at a glance that he was "breaking," and he knew that nothing short of fire will stop a breaking sheep or deer. They have been known to throw themselves over cliffs or to shatter their limbs among boulders when in this state of blind panic. Now Corrie shot past, leaping high into the air, then raced madly on towards the river.

Not far ahead was the millrace, a deep, walled channel built to gather in half the water of the river and send it coursing swiftly down to the huge waterwheel. Corrie was racing straight towards it. When he reached its vertical brink he made no attempt to stop, but simply leaped straight out, to be whirled away by the racing waters. Here was tragedy in the making; there was no way of escaping until he was carried to the end of the channel, where the giant buckets of the turning wheel would pick him up and hurl him into the depths of the pool below.

Now Alastaire himself "broke," or something very near to it, for little short of fire would have stopped him. His only hope of saving Corrie lay in grabbing him immediately the great wheel emptied its buckets into the pool—or that was his wild plan. It was a matter of seconds now, and Alastaire also ran as he had never run before, past the old mill building with its groaning wheel, then down the stone steps to the edge of the pool.

It was a sinister place of profound depth, and black as ink save where the pathways of foam wound across it. Alastaire knew well its terrible undercurrents, for he had taken more than one salmon from its waters. He knew that once a fish got below you the only thing was to put down your rod and snap the line, for he was sure to pass down into the torrent below and scream your reel empty.

The first Alastaire saw of Corrie was when the wheel tossed him headlong across the pool like a saturated sack. But it was Corrie all right. The boy just glimpsed his big ears, then his slender hind legs rising stiffly above the surface.

It was foolish, of course, for what was the life of a deer calf compared with that of a sound Highland boy, yet Alastaire's courage never wavered. He slipped his kilt-buckle, then struck out hand over hand across the pool. Something whispered to him, "Keep on the surface. Don't let your legs sink or you'll be sucked under."

Alastaire was a strong boy for his age and an able swimmer. Fortunately he did not see the miller's wife racing down the steps after him, nor did he hear her horrified screams. He remembered only the incredible sport of it, the fight with the currents, the triumph of catching Corrie by his collar, then the desperate fight to the bank with his heavy load, and the first dawning of fear as he felt himself being borne irresistibly towards the mouth of the caldron. But he did not let Corrie go.

At the very brink the old woman caught him by one arm and hung on, but she could not pull him out and screamed to him to let go of the deer calf. But Alastaire was deaf to her entreaties, and it was not till the miller himself came down that the two were dragged from the water. The old lady embraced the boy about the neck and dissolved into tears of thankfulness, but he said simply, "Thank you, Mary. You did well to hang on to us." He took up his tattered old kilt and rebuckled it, then turned to the miller and said, "Will you carry Corrie for me, John? I'm worn out after that."

The old man looked at the deer calf which had so nearly sunk his employer's son, and shook his head sadly. "No use, Master Alastaire," said he. "He went over the wheel. Every bone in his body must be broken. He's dead—quite dead!"

"Never mind," replied Alastaire. "Please carry him up for me. We must take him back to my sister."

So the solemn little procession went up to the

castle, Alastaire, dripping water, then old John carrying Corrie, and last of all Mary, still shedding tears of thankfulness.

They laid Corrie by the kitchen fire, where the cook covered him with a hot blanket, then Fiona came. Alastaire looked up at her defeatedly and half-accusingly. "It's no use, Fiona," he stammered. "I did my best to save him, but he went over the mill wheel, and he's dead, quite dead."

But Fiona, with eyes only for her brother, threw her eager arms about his neck. "Oh, poor Alastaire! Poor Alastaire!" she cried. "I am sure you did your very best."

Perhaps—who knows?—it was one of the greatest moments in Alastaire's life, for therein he saw his little sister as he would always remember her— a great and gracious lady, who, though her own heart must have been breaking, put that aside for a kindly word to a boy who had done his best.

Because he did not like to see the sadness of others Alastaire went away to one of those quiet corners he knew, to the Singing Forest where the great trees rubbed against each other in the wind and filled the cathedral quietude with a soothing melody. Fiona and her mother remained by the kitchen fire where the soft red light cast its shadows on the pathetic bundle within the circle of warmth, Corrie, with only his pretty little head out of the folds of the blanket with which cook had covered him. They said nothing, because there was nothing to say, nothing to do. Callum had been in and looked at Corrie and touched his eyes, then turned away lest his emotions betray him.

Then in strolled Bongo, staring and sniffing, and thrusting his way to the fire he began to lick Corrie. Lick, lick, lick his pink tongue went from end of the cold little body and back again. He tried to turn him over till ready hands did it for him, and lick, lick, lick Bongo went over the other side. Thirty minutes passed, an hour, but still Bongo licked. He never paused, never looked up from the task he had set himself. He lay down beside Corrie, one yellow paw over the little animal's shoulders as though to warm him, and still he steadily licked on.

Then suddenly Fiona rose with a cry of joy. "Mother—Mother—he's alive!" she cried. "I saw his eyelids flicker! Corrie's alive! Bongo has licked him back to life!"

And she ran through the house, crying triumphantly, "Corrie's alive! Corrie's alive!"

CHAPTER 3

An hour later Corrie ate an enormous meal of boiled cabbage and potato, followed by a whole ginger-cake that the cook had just baked. The next day he was the same Corrie once more, save that he was never again disrespectful to old MacDiarmid; and perhaps he was a little changed in spirit, possibly because he had at last learned fear, which had brought him another stage nearer to the truly wild animal. He still stuck close to the heels of his companions, but he began to show a certain indifference towards their games. He was inclined suddenly to go off on his own with an absent-minded air of independence, and it soon became obvious that his period of infant mischievousness was past. He spent more and more time on the bracken slope behind the mowed castle lawn, and often seemed ill at ease and watchful, as though suspicious of the presence of enemies hitherto unknown.

That his wild instincts were keenly awake was proved by an incident that occurred late that summer. An impenetrable wall of wet mist came driving in from the east, and with the wind behind him and his coat spangled Corrie took up his station in the center of the putting-green and stood staring out towards the bracken field. For ten minutes he stood there, motionless as a statue, save for the semaphoring of his ears and an occasional step forward. So far as human eyes were concerned the visibility was not more than twenty feet in that direction, yet clearly Corrie was *looking* at something—looking at something downwind, so that his nostrils could have given no guidance. He ignored Callum who passed quite near, and Callum decided that according to the way of his kind he was "watching spooks."

When the mist cleared the cause of his curiosity was revealed. The farmer had that day turned an old grey mare into the field, and in the act of rolling she had got on her back in a hollow and been unable to rise. She lay with her belly facing heavenwards and her legs kicking. All Corrie could have seen was this unfamiliar view of the old lady, so no wonder he had stood and stared!

But the mystery was how Corrie *could* have seen her at all in such an atmosphere. The old mare was two hundred yards away, and it seemed incredible that he could have scented her against the wind. The laird held the view that deer can see through the mountain mists which so frequently obscure their high haunts; for many times he had tried to stalk them under cover of it, only to see them a mile away looking back at him when the air cleared.

At all events the laird was sufficiently interested to put the problem before Ewen when he called in that evening with his customary report and for his dram. Ewen at first shook his head, then opening out a little he said: "Well, sir, you will call to mind that some years ago I was stalking for Sir Alfred Gillamorn, the famous eye specialist, and after we'd failed to stalk a herd in the mist, and saw them looking back, he telt me, sir—and these are his very words—that the eyes of such animals are not so very different from our own, but they can open their pupils wider and so let in more light. This, he explained, would not help them to see through mist any more than a stronger light would help us to see through a stone wall."

"Quite true," agreed the laird, "but how did Sir Alfred explain the deer moving off and looking back at him?"

"Well, sir, he said that though they can't see through mist much better than we can, they can scent upwind when the mist is down, because the scent travels along the waves of moisture, just as otter-hounds can scent an otter downstream of them."

Meantime Callum had entered to make his daily report and to take *his* dram.

"That's all right," the laird admitted, "but Corrie this morning was standing and staring at the old mare not because he could smell her, but because there was something unusual in her position. She was, in fact, belly upwards, and therefore presented a mystery to him. In other words, he must have been using his eyes rather than his nose, which knocks Sir Alfred's theory on the head—doesn't it, Callum?"

But Callum, too, was guarded. These were technical fineries hardly for the likes of him. "Well, sir, I am thinking father may be working along the right lines," he ventured. "You'll agree that with deer it is generally a matter of scent, and we know that an alarmed animal gives off a stronger and a different scent than it normally would. Deer smell fear from one to another, and while Corrie would have taken no notice of the old mare in the ordinary way, it would seem that he knew from the smell of her that she was in trouble of some kind out there, and that was what held him." And that seemed about as far as they could get in solving the problem.

Not long afterwards Corrie again distinguished himself, but in quite a different way. A Continental gentleman of some standing was visiting the castle. He was a keen angler and the laird was anxious to show him what could be done in Scottish waters. Toward evening Callum and his father had the boat ready by the shore of the loch below the village, but the sky was bright and the fish would not rise to the lure. Up to the darkening only a four-pound ferox rewarded their efforts, so they turned to the shoal water among the islands in the hope of finding the sea trout. Here their guest almost immediately hooked something that went off in the slow, irre-sistible manner of a heavy fish. "Keep a check on him, sir," advised Callum. "He hasn't wakened up yet, but when he does he may make straight for the overhanging timber."

From the way the fish moved off it looked as

though they might be there till midnight, for their visitor was trolling a very long line, and the deepening darkness would add difficulties to the playing of such a fish among the islands. Their guest was soon standing up in the boat while the laird held tight to his jacket. He was shouting excited instructions to Ewen with the oars, and one might have sworn the old gillie shot a covert wink at the laird. Inexorably, the leviathan swam on towards the point of the island, where they could just make out the heavy swirl of him, though he never seemed to break surface. The visitor shouted excitedly that he was down to his backing, while still his reel continued to scream, and in spite of Ewen's efforts to keep the boat clear of the island, the line was soon sawing dangerously through the lower branches. Then the swirls of the monster disappeared round the point and the position became hopeless. Down went the rod, and with a final scream of anguish from the reel back came the line with a resounding ping as it parted. Their guest sank exhausted to his seat while exclamations of sympathy broke from his companions.

The laird and his men agreed that it would have been the record fish of the season, and long would their guest remember it, and be able to recall the titanic struggle to his friends across the Channel. Certainly he knew now what kind of fish exist in Scottish waters!

When they reached home Corrie was at the garden gate to meet them. "The little devil must have swum after us," whispered the laird to Callum. "Remove that spinner and piece of line from his flank or it will give the whole show away!"

Corrie often went off on exploits of his own, particularly during the night, and on this account Callum unfastened the buckle of his red collar and tied the two ends with string. Thus he would not accidentally hang himself if the collar caught up; moreover, the string would break if the collar became too tight as he grew. Someone suggested attaching a Swiss cowbell, but Callum pointed out that with such an adornment his wild relations would never take to him if he decided to join them—an event to be expected any day now.

And it would not be too soon, for he had almost ceased to be a children's pet, and shortly after the fishing incident he one day, in frolicsome mood, held up a party of hikers and cyclists on the walled road above the bridge. Standing in the middle of the road shaking his head he refused to let them pass, till eventually the "schoolmarm," an elderly spin-

5 1

ster, approached on her cycle from the opposite direction. Ringing her bell and commanding Corrie to go home and behave himself, she tried to get by, at which Corrie reared up on his hind legs and came down with his fore-hoofs on her shoulders. With lady and cycle down in the road the men rallied to her aid and by dint of much "shooing" and hand-kerchief-waving Corrie was driven to the top of the wall, whence he raced home still defiantly shaking his head.

An angry deputation followed him and were met in the avenue by Callum, who reassured them by saying that the deer calf was "no but a wee bit children's pet," and that they should just have boxed his ears and sent him about his business. The visitors pointed out that the lady who had tried to interfere had not proved singularly successful, but after a good deal of repartee on both sides the party broke up quite merrily.

Still it would not do for Corrie to be allowed to make a public nuisance of himself, and the sooner he went the better. Food was still plentiful about the woods and on the moors, though in a few weeks' time the trees would be leafless and winter upon the land. The homing instincts of deer are well known, and Callum held that it would be no use turning him down anywhere on the estate, since he would be home within a few hours; but the laird decided to risk it, saying that after a day or two among the other deer Corrie would become as wild as any of them.

So it was decided to take Corrie into stag country on the other side of the Corrie Rou. This meant a very wide circuit round the end of the range, though as the eagle flies the point at which they proposed to put him down would not be more than twelve miles. Arrangements were made, but before the day of the actual departure Corrie again distinguished himself —for the first time rising to the level of a hero.

On warm sunny days it was customary for the nurse to place the youngest of her charges on a large sheepskin rug in the center of the lawn, there, well bolstered with cushions, to kick her legs in the sun. Bongo as usual was left in charge, and the old lady did not notice Corrie standing rigidly at attention in the angle of the barn wall, and had she done so it would have conveyed nothing.

Five minutes later the defensive barking of Bongo, to which Chang lent the thunder of his growls and the majesty of his support, brought the nurse to an upstairs window, and there she saw Corrie standing up on his hind legs alongside the baby, and obviously in danger of trampling her when he came down. Nanny squealed to Mac-Diarmid who was working near, but ere the gardener could reach the place there was a terrific swish of wings as an eagle came down and passed over the child almost within reach of Corrie's thrashing fore-hoofs.

It was an ugly moment; for though the great bird of prey could hardly have carried the child away, it might have dragged her and clawed her badly had not Corrie been there. He, undoubtedly, was the hero; for poor old Bongo, never expecting danger from overhead, merely fell over backwards, while Chang headed pell-mell for the cucumber frames and, to judge from the crash of glass that followed, safely gained the interior. When MacDiarmid arrived Corrie was still on guard, red-eyed and stamping, but by then the eagle was far back in the heavens.

Never again was the baby placed out on the lawn, and unquestionably there was much for which they had to thank Corrie's wild instincts. He alone knew that the eagle was circling over that one point and had divined its intentions, though whether it was an heroic desire to guard the child or merely his natural hatred of the great bird of prey we can only form our own views.

Though Corrie's shares had gone up with a bound, the necessity for his deportation was in no way lessened, and when the day came he was packed in a large oblong hamper through which he could not see, and this was strapped to the roof of the family car. With Callum at the wheel the whole family except the baby set out on their long journey for a final summer picnic.

On the way Callum chanced to remark to his employer, who was seated in front with him, that on the other side of the range there was a very old woman reputed to possess the second sight. She was close upon a hundred years of age and lived in a cottage at the roadside, and in his boyhood he and his sister had been taken to her to be blessed. He said that many children were taken to her for this holy purpose, and it was very clear what the High-lander had in his mind.

The laird opened the sliding window between the front seat and the back, and explained that Callum thought the two children should be taken on the way to receive the old lady's blessing. Their mother was wholeheartedly in favor. Fiona thought it might prove a novel experience, but Alastaire was not particularly keen. He thought it would be more to the mark if she blessed Corrie, since it was really he who was starting out on his life's adventures; in fact, while they were at it, the entire lot of them might as well be blessed. He was sure his daddy stood as much in need of it as he did, at which his mother mildly rebuked him. To take such a ceremony lightly would be a slight to the old lady they were about to visit, with which he quite reasonably concurred.

They arrived at the door of what was little more than a hut, and since Callum could speak her dialect of Gaelic, he headed the procession, the family following. The old lady proved to be rather blind and not a little deaf, but she knew at once why the children had been brought, and bade them remain at the door till she was ready. Soon she reappeared, transformed in all the splendor of her Highland lace, and very lovingly and reverently she blessed them both, placing her hands upon their heads.

She breathed her blessing on the boy first, and he would never forget the strange thrill it gave him. Her bony old fingers on his hair seemed to send a tingle of strength through all his being, while her soft voice gave him new peace and contentment. He would now have been the last to scoff at an old woman's blessings.

She called him by his Christian names, Alastaire Roy, and bade him be brave, for he would have to face many perils with his clansmen against the forces of evil. He must never be afraid, for fear was the cause of all war, of poverty, and of most humiliation and suffering. She seemed to endow him with the protection of her own many years by the pressure of her hand on his fair hair, while his mother mopped her eyes and his father sniffed and Callum stood by, rigid as a poker. When Fiona's turn came she, too, the old lady called by her Christian names, Fiona Morag. She blessed the little girl's love affairs —for they, alas, would be many—her marriage and her own dear children. Fiona felt herself growing like a mushroom from childhood to womanhood, but with a woman's happy cares only, echoing down the primrose paths she was yet to tread; after which the old lady blessed the happiness of their remaining childhood and youth together.

It was a fine little ceremony, and anxious to postpone the closing of it Fiona eagerly interposed the suggestion that Corrie also should be blessed. The old lady could not understand the child's eager entreaty or the clutch of her fingers on her arm, so

Callum was called upon to interpret, which he did gravely and sincerely.

The old lady laughed, the hamper was lifted down from the roof of the car, and Corrie was blessed through the lid of it—that he might not fall to the hand of man nor yet to his wild enemies, but finally to the more kindly hand of Time.

When they went on they asked Callum how she had known the children's Christian names, for the high hills shut off one glen from the next and in her infirm state she could not have known who they were. But this question Callum could not answer, nor any other body, for she always knew the Christian names of children taken to her. And to think that but a few years ago such a woman would have been dreaded and damned as a witch!

At the end of nearly three hours' driving they stopped the car at the head of a tidal loch, and all of them—including Bongo and Chang—were transferred with the hamper and the lunch basket to a rowboat. On the other side they pitched their camp and the picnic lunch was set out on the moss. Corrie was released from his prison and given a whole loaf of gingerbread, then the laird and Callum returned to the water to fish for sea trout while the others wandered into the valley of the little burn which climbed steeply into the hills. A herd of young stags grazed peacefully on the slope above, and sea swallows flew creeking and chattering in the sunshine. The last they saw of Corrie was when he was far above them, nosing among the ferns and the remaining flowers in a mossy dell, his red collar conspicuous from afar. So they stole away and left him to the fortunes of his own life among his own kind.

The journey home was not quite so radiant. Back in the boat Bongo did his best to point out that they had left Corrie behind, and would have jumped overboard had not Alastaire clung tightly to his collar. While they were crossing the end of the range the mountain mists came down, and the old car seemed to lumber on eternally. Then it began to rain and Fiona started crying, so that it was the wettest journey imaginable. Alastaire and Callum did their best to cheer the proceedings by singing Gaelic songs.

It was raining hard in their own valley, and as darkness fell prematurely another disconcerting thing happened. Bongo could not be found, either about the grounds or in the village, and they had to shut down for the night without him. But Callum was grinning from ear to ear.

Next morning, when the laird was shaving in his dressing room, he heard Bongo's lazy old bark on the lawn below, and looking out he saw him seated on the dewy lawn gazing eagerly upwards. He was covered with mud and looked like an oiled seagull, but his expression clearly said, "Now aren't I a clever dog?" For during the night Bongo had been over the hills and far away, and now at his side stood an equally muddy Corrie, safely shepherded home over the highlands.

🌿 🌿 🌿

CHAPTER 4

In that easygoing family the question of Corrie's transportation seemed now to slip into the background, and soon the dawns of the Indian summer were touched with frost. The rowan trees began to reflect their memories of summer sunsets, and the quivering leaves of the birch trees were falling to earth in golden showers. Corrie was slowly and surely leaving home in his own way, so why not leave him to it and avoid all heartaches? In the early mornings he would always appear at Fiona's call, but at other times of the day it was not so certain. She was not sad about it, because she understood that he had outgrown the period of being a children's pet, and this was the natural order. His hearing must have been very keen, for if at any time she persisted in calling he would eventually arrive panting, indicating that he had come far and fast to her summons. Sometimes he walked sedately through the village street, his head alertly uplifted as though he himself were the laird of the glen, and one thing was certain—that neither stray dogs nor cats visited the castle these days.

The red deer are a silent lot and do not call to each other as fox calls to fox, or as the buzzards call to each other across the width of the skies. For ten months of the year they are the least vociferous of all wild animals, their only vocal intercourse consisting of the occasional barking of the hinds, the bleat of a calf, or the grunt of an ill-humored stag. Then in October the big stags move to the terraces, and for so long as the rut lasts they make up for the long period of voicelessness.

So the night came when there sounded from the ridges and the washouts, the corries and the screes, the high bugling of the king stags coming down from the Corrie Rou. They came from the vast hinterlands which lie beyond, from the haunts of fox and wildcat and ptarmigan, and their bugling was answered by the hoarse challenging of other stags far and near. This deep valley to which they were descending was a more kindly region than the stony heights they were leaving, crossed and crisscrossed for three thousand feet above the river with deep little valleys, many of them densely wooded. Then, too, there were the vast Forestry Commission plantings, affording shelter for deer as for vermin of many kinds, for even these sacred areas cannot be made deer-proof; one cannot keep deer out when frozen snow piles up to the top of the highest deer fences.

This was hind country as distinct from stag country over the heights, and on these sheltered slopes the hinds nursed their calves and found shelter from the winter storms. Here the great Corrie Rou itself predominated. It was stupendous to the point of being terrifying. The cliffs rose a sheer thousand feet over the deep cutting into the face of the mountain, two miles across—though, since there was nothing with which to compare it, it looked less. In those cliffs the eagle, the raven, the peregrine and the buzzard nested; it was a haunt of outlaws inaccessibly dug in among the screes and along the shelves. Sometimes silence reigned, sometimes a single wild cry sent a thousand echoes re-echoing eerily. At one time illicit stills worked in its recesses—"at one time" we say, for that is a useful term in the Highlands where there will always be lawless men. There the wild goats still live, and a herd of little red deer hold the high ridges and shelter in the washouts, rarely seen by man. It is said that they never exceed one hundred and fifty pounds in weight or ten points, but they are agile and swift, and graze from perilous footholds to which the heavier deer never climb. One comes to love such places as the Corrie Rou, but in times of storm one shrinks from their cruelty.

From the basin of the Corrie the mountain falls steeply to the river, but here again there is many a plateau and many a washout hidden from the valley below. There is the level swamp where we first met Corrie, and below that the Green Braes where we shall meet him later. The village lies beyond the ridge, and below it the loch of many islands. Farther away is the Singing Forest, from which the land rises steadily again through scattered pine to the grouse moors, and beyond that again more hinterlands, more deer forests. But the deer are rarely known to cross from valley to valley, those of the north side being a different people from those of the Corrie Rou.

This, then, was the land of Corrie's heritage, and from the bracken field behind the castle he heard that autumn the wild music of his own kind. It went down to his soul like the skirl of the pipes to the exiled Highlander, thrilling every sense of him and bidding him go where he belonged. He had never before heard the roaring of the stags, but he knew it instinctively. Then he began to move, slowly, step by step, but listening the while.

He was like a creature mesmerized. Slowly, stride by stride, he went, down to the road and towards the bridge of many arches. He had crossed it many times before, but tonight, in the starlight, he chose a different way. He left the road and passed on upstream till he reached a point at which an island stood in the middle of the river, for here was the age-old crossing-place of his kind—*they* never crossed by the bridge. So, for the first time since his infancy, tonight he was a truly *wild* deer, and on their appointed highway.

It was a beautiful island, cleaving the river clean in two, with foaming cataracts either side of it, and it lay there like a destroyer in a stormy sea. A ridge of stately pine trees ran the length of it, some of the tallest in the land, for all the sunshine was overhead and drew them up. The river itself was almost eternally in shadow, and the island was beautiful in its tumbled chaos because it had never known the restraining hand of the forester.

Here was the recognized deer-crossing. By this way the hinds brought their calves to raid the slopes of the upper strath, and Corrie chose to cross by their own footholds—here a hollow in the smooth rock face where thousands had placed their hoofs before him, there a narrow leap with a boiling channel below. So Corrie gained the island where the scent of his kind was faint among the wet verdure. The other side was shallow and he bounded across easily, up the steep bank and into the clover field to the main road, so that if he had crossed by the bridge he would have saved all this detour. But tonight Corrie was treading the chosen pathways of his kind, as hitherto he had trodden his chosen pathways about the castle garden.

Back near the bridge a white iron gate led through to the occupation road which followed the river on the south side, and so on eventually to Ewen's lodge. By the gate stood the game-keeper's cottage with its rambler roses and vege-table plot, and Corrie slipped between the bars of the gate as nimbly as a roe deer, not even wakening the dogs in the kennels.

This was the Big Wood, or rather the beginning of it, and the occasional roaring and belling of stags echoed among the trees.

As yet few of the big stags from over the Heights had settled on the terraces; they were still in process of whipping in their herds, but already settled in the woods were a few outlying greyface stags more or less resident there. It was evidently for one of these herds that Corrie was heading. He left the road and climbed higher into the wood till he reached a sequestered hollow where stood the ruins of a clachan, whose broken walls provided a shelter such as deer love. Ferns grew from the walls and shrubs and willowherb occupied the tiny rooms. Regularly the deer sheltered there, hollowing out their harbors to the curvature of the bodies in the protected corners.

Resident deer will always find such quarters, but as Corrie stole silently up, there was no sign of his own kind. The moon was now up, and the whole great wood a jig-saw of moonlight and shadow. Man would not have believed that less than sixty feet away was a strong herd of deer, for they were all lying down, chewing the cud, and save for a questing glance they paid no heed to the little wraith of the moonlight who had clearly come to join them.

Corrie stood with ears laid back, nervously awaiting an invitation. He could see the grey faces of the resting hinds all turned towards him, and he could feel their dark eyes fixed upon him. Some of them had calves resting under them, and after a while one of the hinds rose, stretched herself, then came swiftly towards him. She was an old animal, but in perfect condition, for her coat had something of the gloss of sable. She was, in fact the grandmother of the clan, and was so well groomed because her children and her grandchildren were forever licking her.

Her rising was the general signal and most of them got up and stretched themselves. Corrie stood stock-still while the old hind sniffed his face and his ears and his neck till she came to the red collar, then she thrust him impatiently aside. Others of the hinds and some of the calves came up to gather round him in a ring, and all of them sniffed him till they came to the red collar, then they, too, thrust him aside. So he was shuttled from one to another till he found himself among the calves, and one of them, a little hind calf of his own age, had a white star on her forehead. She seemed inclined to tolerate him in spite of his Sassenach adornment, for she invited him to play, but just then there was a challenging roar which veritably shook the forest giants to their roots.

Next moment an enormous grey-faced stag stepped out from one of the roofless buildings. He looked double the size of any of the hinds. His horns spread from his broad forehead like the branches of an oak, for he was a Royal, in fact an Imperial, a fourteen-pointer. His back was humped and his neck was swollen, and he stepped forth from his harbor like some grim despot of an earlier world. Yet Corrie was unafraid in his majestic presence, and in truth the big stag had not yet noticed the little newcomer.

The Imperial stood in the moonlight listening, then he began to bark and to rumble, pawing at the ground and tossing the fallen leaves over his shoulders. Clearly he had sensed the approach of a rival, and presently he darted off towards a bramble thicket in the hollow at the foot of the beech knoll; and from the other side of the thicket crashed another big stag who had crept up unseen to within striking distance of the herd.

He, too, was a Royal, but his horns were set

close together, rising almost vertically, and appeared to be crowded with short points. He was a yellowface from over the mountains.

He went off as though for his life at the approach of the big greyface, but he was cunning, inviting pursuit. He invited the greyface almost to overtake him, then suddenly he doubled back while his rival overshot. Thus the raider was between the greyface and his herd, and the next moment the trespassing stag was thundering towards the clachan. Thus he scattered the herd of hinds in all directions, his object being to cut out some of them.

The calves with their mothers seemed to regard it as an immense joke. Some of them jumped to the tops of the crumbling walls, and there was little Starpoint on the topmost pinnacle shaking her woolly head with an air of impudent defiance.

But Corrie was not up to the game, and sought refuge in flight. The result was that when the rightful master of the herd had restored order Corrie was eighty yards away, standing alone in an open glade, with the yellowface raider between him and the herd. To regain the others he would somehow have to get round the savage yellowface.

Savage he was, for his ruse had failed, and he

was still hindless. He began to paw the ground, roaring continuously, while the greyface acted in like manner between him and the flustered hinds. Corrie thought he saw his chance and tried to double back, but the yellowface saw him and with a bound intercepted him. Next moment Corrie was fleeing for his life with the stag thundering behind him, striving to throw him into the air to satisfy his own ill mood.

Corrie headed for home—down the wood towards the river. The gradient handicapped his heavy pursuer on the soft footing, while Corrie could dodge in and out among the hazels and brambles like a blob of mercury. He clattered across the occupation road where the big stag skidded and almost fell, but next moment the yellowface had him pinioned at the river margin and Corrie had to cross where he was.

He meant in any case to put running water between himself and his foe, but this was not the point at which any deer would have chosen to cross. He had to plunge straight into deep water, and but for his native instincts he would have received a very bad ducking. Those instincts bade him swim with the current, not to fight it, and in a few seconds he was yards away. This was the channel into which the mill-pool drained—the very pool that had so nearly claimed him and Alastaire a few weeks ago.

At the first possible landing place on the other side Corrie scrambled ashore. He looked back across the angry waters, but could see nothing of the stag under the trees. He shook himself and the spray flew far and wide in the moonlight. One shake and he was dry; it was a process by which the red deer stay alive, and it was well so, for the frost was now keen.

No doubt Corrie had seen enough of the Wild for one night. High in the woods across the river he could still hear the roaring and thrashing of the stags. Probably the donkey-eared yellowface had returned to taunt the big greyface. Not far away, beyond the twinkling lights of the village, was home, and his own deep bed in the summer house waiting to receive him. So in that direction Corrie hurried.

The rutting season was brief and fierce, and hard on its heels came winter. By mid-November most of the big stags were back over the Corrie Rou, and ice and snow gripped the land to the river margins.

Callum was living with his parents at the

stalker's lodge at the end of the occupation road until a cottage became vacant for him and his young wife. He came and went by motorcycle, and the rough little road was ice-coated that November night.

Riding cautiously he was within half a mile of home when he distinctly heard the clatter of hoofs on the road and in the wood on either side. A herd of deer were evidently stampeding in front of him, and it was some seconds before he remembered that just ahead an old deer fence ran down to the river, forming the march between the hardwood and the spruce plantings. On reaching this the herd he was pursuing would be forced to turn back to meet him, and he at once realized the danger. He stopped his machine, and sure enough he was just in time to see the deer returning, packed together, their eyes reflecting the glare of his headlamp across the middle of the road.

Of all wild animals, hill deer are among the most perilous to meet after dark, and that for the very natural reason that they have no road sense. They seem quite incapable of judging the speed of an oncoming vehicle, or even the direction in which it is traveling. They are as likely to jump into it as to jump in the opposite direction, and when dazzled by lights they have no judgment of any kind. The herd ahead was like a flock of moths held by a candle.

Callum groped for his light-switch, but for the life of him he could not find it, and as the rumble of hoofs drew nearer he had no alternative but to grab the cap from his head and thrust it over the headlight. Next moment there was a crash, followed by blows which beat the blood into his eyes.

When he came to he was lying at the side of the road. His machine lay in the middle of it some feet away. He felt as though every bone in his body were broken, but he managed to get to his feet, and feeling himself over he was unable to find any damage except for bruises and abrasions. The headlamp was still alight, and going over to the machine he managed to jack it on to its stand. Here, too, little damage was done save for bent handlebars and footrests and a few minor fractures. All the same he decided to leave the machine where it stood and to walk home.

Not till then did he see the big greyface stag lying in the road not ten yards away. Leading the herd, it was probably he who had first crashed into the machine, and quite clearly he was very badly shaken—perhaps disabled. His head was up and he was still staring in a bewildered manner at the light, so Callum switched it off lest he should again crash into it.

It is not wise to approach too near a cornered stag, so Callum threw snowballs at the poor old fellow to see if he could arouse him. Eventually he scrambled to his legs, and after a good deal of slipping and sliding ambled stiffly off into the trees. There appeared to be no bones broken, but he was pretty far run and was badly shaken up, possibly injured internally. And this was the big Royal which had held his hinds by the ruins in the forest, and which Callum's father declared was the father of Corrie of Corrie Rou!

It is strange how things pan out; for with the coming of the frost Fiona had taken to carrying hay into the bracken field for Corrie, and two mornings later there was the big greyface feeding near Corrie. He was very stiff and lame; sick deer quickly lose their fear of human beings. As Fiona entered the field the stag ambled off, but no farther than to the top wall, where he stood watching. Fiona laid down a double ration of hay, and no sooner was she back at the gate than the greyface came down and he and Corrie fed together. The news that the old stag was the father of Corrie —and the children now took that as accepted— added a further romance to the story, and certainly he was welcome to all the food and shelter they could give him.

Soon the big stag did not trouble to retreat when anyone entered the field, and began to feed while they stood by. At that stage Callum forbade Fiona to carry hay for them. Even with the best intentions in the world it was not safe for a small person to go too near; for a single sweep of those spreading antlers might have dire consequences. Callum himself kept his hay fork ready when feeding the animals; for, encouraged by Corrie, the stag was not opposed to snatching a mouthful of hay even from his arms. He was perfectly docile and well meaning, but he had no knowledge of his own strength, which was well illustrated when one day he had a slight difference of opinion with the gate to the field, and forthwith lifted it clean over his shoulders.

Thus another dependent was added to their ménage, and all that long winter Corrie and Greyface lived in the bracken field together. With the first breath of spring Callum began to cut down their hay ration, for with the young green grass springing in the hollows it was high time both of them returned to the forest. Concurrently, the big stag's horns became loose, and could be seen to wobble while he fed. The movement apparently irritated him, till one morning he shook his head violently, whereupon one of the horns flew yards, and hit Corrie on the face. Having overcome his surprise and indignation Corrie at once began to gnaw the points in search of the calcium his body needed, but Callum took the great horn from him and later collected the other to show to the laird. They indicated that the big beast was already past his prime, for there was the beginning of decay in the antler tips. This stag should be put off the ground before next roaring season.

Corrie's own first points now began to appear, but their growth did not seem to trouble him much, whereas Greyface was destined to go sore-headed for many weeks, and not till after mid-summer would his new horns be free of blood and velvet.

Corrie had put on weight during the winter, and was now a tall, sturdy little knobber, bearing every promise of becoming a fine stag. Assuredly no hill beast had ever stood a better chance by way of good feeding during calfhood, and it is that which builds up the frame for all time. But old Greyface had not flourished of late, and was clearly ready for a few weeks of rich mountain grazing— or maybe his huge frame lacked some chemical about which his instincts had begun to warn him.

It is at this season, immediately after casting, that the heaviest mortality occurs among hill stags. A few hinds may die in the early spring from overeating, but old stags die wholesale at this time, many through heart failure, others because winter finds them all too unready to meet it, so that by the end of the cold months their strength is gone. Their carcasses strew the hillsides of every great forest, and their bodies are carried into the valleys by the torrents that take the salmon downstream.

The two deer left the bracken field at night time, and there could be no doubt that Corrie had at last gone for good. He had gone with his father, not as father and son, but rather as master and boy. Greyface would lead, and it was simply for Corrie to follow.

So the days of Corrie as a children's pet ended, and he went forth to the hills to live the normal life of the forests. Other changes at the castle were

pending too, for that Easter the son of the house
would leave the village school to go to boarding
school. According to the custom of Highland
lairds' children, he had hitherto received his learn-
ing among those who would serve him in later
life, that they might know each other at least as
children together.

Old Ewen MacEwen was due for retirement,
and Callum would become head stalker. Ewen
might hobble round with the master another
season or two, for it was unthinkable that their
long partnership should be abruptly ended, but
Ewen was a very old man, and the war had not
prolonged the youth of either of them.

Under a roof of low-flung stars Greyface and
Corrie crossed the big swamp where Corrie's mother
had fallen, and at daybreak they were far out on
the desolate marshlands that fill the lower portion
of the valley for thirty miles to the sea. This was
an area man had never attempted to reclaim, a
great unfertile desolation of heather and marshes,
deeply eaten into by the floods, a region of curlew
and snipe and redshank, whose voices during these
spring days filled the whole area with doleful
melody.

Corrie wanted to dally and to fill his belly at

the many green patches they passed, but Greyface bore relentlessly on, clearly bent on some far distant goal. Several times they swam the river where it crossed their path, winding from side to side of the great delta, and always the procedure was the same. On nearing the water Corrie would clap himself to the flank of his big companion, on the downstream side, so that the upward swirl kept him there, and they would cross as though glued together, swimming low in the water with only their heads above the surface. So Corrie would have crossed many a swirling torrent alongside his mother had she lived to shelter him, and instinctively he attached himself in the same way to Greyface, who seemed to be quite unaware of his presence. So far he had completely ignored his small companion, and it was only for Corrie to follow.

That afternoon Greyface lay down under a high flood bank to rest, and Corrie would fain have rested with him save that he was too empty. They had eaten nothing since their last feed of hay, and while Greyface rested, Corrie eagerly nosed about in the rank swamp verdure for a sweet morsel here and there. So intent was he that he did not notice the shepherd with his two dogs working the green slope above, but the shepherd saw him, and he did not welcome the presence of deer, for he had the eatage of that part of the bottom lands. He could not see Greyface, but he could see the stag calf and judged that other deer would be there; so he pointed out Corrie to his dogs, and away they swept to put the deer off the land.

Those dogs were used to working together, and at full speed they quickly covered the intervening mile. Corrie saw only the black-and-white one racing towards him—the other, half a mile on the downstream side, he still did not see. At all events he had come to regard dogs as of little consequence, and he stood upright staring till the black-and-white one was within fifty yards of him. Then his wild instincts awoke. Perhaps he saw that this dog was more terribly intent than any he had met hitherto; perhaps he realized that he was no longer on his own territory and was faced with new danger. Or, perhaps, for the first time in his life, the wolf-fear was thoroughly wakened.

Only just in time did he issue the warning to Greyface by exhaling sharply through his nostrils. The thin stab of sound took Greyface to his legs, and in an instant he was away like the wind, head thrown back, bounding without effort but at tremendous speed. This frightened Corrie, who fell in behind him—swifter than any sheepdog.

But the second dog saw them approaching, and instantly flattened down in the heather to waylay them, while their pursuer yapped lustily to keep their attention behind them. Thus they ran straight into the ambush, and though an immense bound carried Greyface clear of danger, Corrie landed right in the middle of it. That dog almost got him, and had he done so the other would have joined the issue within a few seconds and the story of Corrie's life would have ended here.

Greyface did not wait for him. He might have turned back to fight for his small companion had the scent of Corrie's blood come to his nostrils, but even that is doubtful. He bore straight on out of the danger zone without even a backward glance, leaving the calf to fend for himself. Corrie was a wild deer among wild deer now, a stag among stags, and it was for him to guard his own interests.

So he had to double and twist for his life, and the wolf-fear really came to him. By the time he regained Greyface he had raced five miles and swum the river twice and he was panting heavily.

The dogs had long since given up the chase and Corrie had learned his lesson.

Yet he had another lesson to learn, for Greyface was angry. Corrie clearly had not carried out the duties which devolved upon him—he had been negligent in his watching, and his negligence had led to all this trouble. So Greyface beat him ahead, as an angry horse persecutes another, punishing him anew every time the younger beast allowed him to overtake, and so for another five miles till Corrie was fit to drop.

All this time Corrie's one thought was to keep out of reach of Greyface. He knew that his master was driving him, but he did not know that Greyface was also guiding him—guiding him clear of the bottomless peat holes and quicksands which became more numerous as they neared the sea. They could now taste the sea in the air, and to Corrie, in spite of his discomfiture, it was wholly delectable, though not till the day was far spent did that nightmare journey end. By that time one fact was firmly established in Corrie's mind—that if they were overtaken by danger he would be punished for it, and that therefore it behooved him to keep good watch.

CHAPTER 5

That night, under the stars, with the breath
of the sea in their nostrils, and with the cries of
thousands of duck and waders filling the air,
Greyface and Corrie grazed the banks of a small
circular tarn which the spring tides filled and where
a small plant grew luxuriantly. It grew in bushes
not more than a foot in height, and Corrie soon
learned that if he took firm hold of it, its palmated
sprays stripped away from its hard, fibrous fronds,

leaving his mouth full of a salty, gelatinous sap, bitter yet sweet, luscious yet in a way distasteful. It burned the mouth and the throat, yet warmed the stomach with a new, life-giving fuel. It took the burn from the eyes, and the pains of insufficiency from the stomach, yet two days of it set Corrie longing for fresh green food which would sustain. It scoured their stomachs as only "deer medicine" can, and Corrie became more and more hungry for the green grass of the upper valley, till he could tolerate the craving no longer. He turned his head inland and looked back for Greyface to follow. The old stag ignored him, so again he went on and looked back, but still Greyface was indifferent. Corrie was reluctant to go without his big companion, but his stomach was empty and go he must. He was far in the distance when, looking round, he saw that, slowly and indifferently, Greyface was following.

So it was now Corrie who led and Greyface who followed. They had come by an established deer road, though there was little to indicate it. A road once traversed by a deer, however, is a road forever remembered, and it is as well so, or thousands would perish in the pot-holes and in the torrents —as indeed they do when transported to new

8 6

country. Corrie led the way back almost by the very hoof-marks they had left on the coastward journey three days earlier.

They traveled fast, though repeatedly Corrie had to look back and wait for Greyface. It was thirty miles in a straight line, and the deer path made many detours and involved many river crossings, yet they covered it in six hours. By sundown they had reached the beginning of the Green Braes, where the most desolate of the swamp lands ceased. Here the grass was green, and they fed among the sheep, though they were soon satisfied, for the eating was succulent and sustaining. It was fortunate, indeed, that they did not overeat and then lie down as hinds with following calves are so apt to do.

The two deer had never felt more vigorous, for the salty weed had supplied what their blood needed, particularly to Greyface, who was still restless. He knew the peril of these bottom lands. Grazing steadily in an upstream direction, they came to the great white stone in the middle of the river where the deer cross. The river was in heavy spate owing to the melted snow coming down from the hills—running bank-full and bitterly cold. They were leg-weary, well fed and content, and they lay down under the alders near to the great white stone, round which the rum-colored stream surged with the steely tinkle of waters that would freeze if they stopped flowing.

They slept—but such dreams as came to Corrie! Greyface also dreamed, for repeatedly he grunted and stretched himself and moved into fresh attitudes on his couch. Both knew that this was a bad place for deer to linger. Corrie's dreams were all of the murder of his own kind, with bloody men and bloody wolves in the midst of them. The wolves and the men worked together as they do to this day, and he could hear the shouts and the whistling of the men, while the wolves descended upon him, white-fanged and snarling. It was as though he slept with his eyes open, for he was in the midst of the herds, yet he could see the dark river—could see the white stone in the middle of it, and once he saw men clinging to it while the herds of deer fighting through the water trampled them under. He would waken and look with terrified eyes about him, only to see the world at peace, the twinkling stars, the Green Braes, and the stooping alders clutching at the water. Then the ghost herds would come tramping back, many hundreds of deer from the

Corrie Rou, majestic overhead, and from the hinterlands which lie behind it, with men in the water striking them down, dragging their half-dead bodies ashore, while great herds of men and wolves drove still more to their doom in the deeper water. He heard the world-old hack of steel on bone as those in the water strove to turn back, to be brutally beaten in the faces with clubs and axes, all of it terrifying in its reality, till Corrie could stand it no longer and rose to tap Greyface with a dainty polished fore-hoof. Then Greyface also rose and plunged into the flooded river at the deer-crossing by the white stone.

So they crossed, but they did not dally in the sheep pastures at the bottom of the Green Braes. They went on past the old barn where Ewen kept his Shetland ponies and so into the higher pastures below the great swamp. Here many deer were grazing, all with a watchful eye for the shepherds, for dawn had come. Greyface and Corrie grazed with them, but never again would Corrie dally in the vicinity of the white stone, for he knew that that area was bad. Thus, by his own finding, not by example, would he in future shun that region which the red deer re-gard as a forbidden terrain, for Ewen MacEwen would have told you that the deer never graze in the fields below the old barn.

An ocean storm came with its icy winds and driving sleet, to be followed by the sudden wakening of the eyes of nature to look upon the primroses in the mossy nooks, then the quick step to early summer. For in those northern lands there is no long-lingering caress of spring, and the seasons pass in their stride almost direct from winter to summer.

Corrie and Greyface, still together, slowly grazed their way upwards from the woodlands to the moors. By early summer they were high up on the heathered slopes that lie beyond the valley of the Corrie Rou. The laird called this area his grouse moor, though so far as was known there had only been one covey on it for several years. Every summer there were herds of deer scattered everywhere—badly organized parcels of young stags, but mainly hinds which had calved or were about to calve. They hid in the old heather about the pine ridges, and one could distinguish the nursing mothers from afar by their assumed air of indifference which hid a constant watchfulness. After every few mouthfuls they would raise their heads and look absently all round, but always long and searchingly in one direction, with the result that when five or six were feeding together it was one long succession of heads bobbing up above the heather.

All the stags had their horns still in velvet. They were hot and pulsing, and when disagreement broke out among them they would stand up on their long hind legs and box grotesquely with their fore-hoofs. Such humans as hove in view at this season were of no consequence, a shepherd at his gathering or a keeper going the round of his vermin traps. The deer were completely at peace, though the sight of strange holiday-makers crossing the hill quickly put them off the ground.

The topmost tablelands drained their thousands of acres on to these lower slopes, with the result that they were fissured with watercourses where rowan, hazel and scrub oak afforded abundant shelter for the deer. There were waterfalls and crystal pools, at which no man ever saw the stag at eve drinking his fill, and that for the very good reason that hill deer do not normally drink at all, for throughout the year their pasturage is sodden with moisture. When Corrie and Greyface crossed one of these sparkling torrents they would dip their muzzles, then immediately lift their heads with their mouths dripping, and that is about as much as the average highland stalker ever sees in his lifetime of a stag drinking its fill. On the other hand, deer must keep their noses moist in dry weather, for their keen sense of smell would be useless were it not accompanied by an equally keen sense of wind direction.

But every dawn, as they lay in their dewy harbors, the two deer would see the ptarmigan when they came down from their stony heights to drink, and often they made a pretty picture. As the slanting sunbeams just kissed the tallest sprigs of heather, setting them sparkling with thousands of rainbow jewels, a covey of the Alpine birds would come twisting and banking across the sunbeams, to drop among the patches of silver sand uttering their frog-like croaking on all sides. Then daintily they would reach up to pick the sparkling berries, purple and mauve and mother-of-pearl, stretching their long necks while the camouflage of their plumage stood out sharply against the brown and silver, albeit their own coloring. Soon the sun would send the dewdrops sliding down the strands of gossamer from sprig to sprig, till in the dark hollows they looked like fairy lanterns at a carnival.

Watching Greyface and the other deer Corrie quickly learned the wild telegraphy of the hills. Of all mountain birds the curlews were the feathered sentries of the hills, and their "danger" warnings were unmistakable. But their warnings were full of false alarms so far as the deer were concerned, for what cared the deer for the passing of raven or peregrine or weasel? All the same they knew curlew language and could interpret it to their own uses.

Next to the curlews came the Alpine hares, which were rarely in evidence when all was peaceful, though they were everywhere. A hare moving downhill was of no significance, but two or more hares moving up would bring Corrie to his feet, for hares always move upward when danger threatens. And if Corrie saw other deer searching the skyline he would not lie down till he had ascertained the suspected danger and assured himself that it was past, or of no importance.

Through the weeks of April and May, Greyface and Corrie lived within a mile of one central point on these pleasant slopes, Corrie watchful, Greyface frequently stretched out in the heather in his favorite attitude, one foreleg extended, the other tucked under him. Most of their harbors were under the sheltering screes or the gravel banks, but there was one sunny place at which none of the deer ever rested—namely, under the cliffs of Mam Shiel.

The great cliff rose several hundred feet, forming the topmost barrier of this range. Its rugged brow was their skyline, and at the foot of the cliff lay a bewilderment of boulders, among which were littered the bleached bones of deer. This was not to be wondered at, for young beasts were given to exploring its shelves and chimneys, which were composed largely of soft earth in which the rocks were set. The plateau above drained over the face of it, so that its shelves were always dripping, and since higher up these were ice-bound till well into early summer, the warming sun was forever sending landslides, large and small, clattering from above. Therefore, to have lain at the foot of it would have meant the danger of being pelted or even buried.

Early spring brought a concentration of thunderstorms towards the magnetic center of Corrie Rou, and since it was Corrie's first experience of thunder on the open hills he made an arrant fool of himself. As the din grew nearer he began to run wildly in all directions, till finally he lay down on the dry bed of a washout, clapped to the earth like a terrified rabbit. With the first downpour a wall of water descended into the washout, and Corrie was swept downstream and would have been drowned but that he was thrown up at an easy landing place. Having scrambled out he wriggled deep down into the roots of a patch of old heather, wet and cold, and there he remained for two terrible hours while the storm crashed and rumbled in all directions. Old Greyface lay between two boulders, calmly chewing his cud. On one of the boulders another experienced veteran of the hill, an old cock grouse, sat with feathers compressed allowing the water to stream from his tail tip. One shake and he was dry, for they were children of the same environment, and in many ways their habits were the same.

Between the storms, flashes of sunshine vividly revealed where the deer were, for as the sun shone out little haloes of light appeared here and there. The deer themselves were invisible against the dark earth, but as each rose and shook itself it threw an iridescent circle of raindrops from its coat, so that for a few seconds the whole vast slope was dotted with this will-o'-the-wisp effect. Anyone watching would indeed have wondered that there could be so many deer hidden away in the hollows where the binoculars would never have revealed them.

When it was all over Corrie crawled miserably out. The air remained hot and heavy and the midges appeared in dense clouds, and not only midges but other biting flies, which were soon tormenting the deer beyond all endurance. Among them was a fly which had the unpleasant habit of swooping into their nostrils, disturbing them greatly, though it did not bite them. It merely laid its eggs there, and when some days later the grubs hatched out, these would cause considerable irritation, resulting in running eyes and noses, the symptoms being similar to those of hay fever. In this uncomfortable state the infected beast would remain till the grubs were finally squeezed out, to assume a fresh phase of life. No lasting harm was done, but such are the parasites which attack the wild creatures living their lives beyond the aid of man.

In all directions the deer now began to stream over the ridges, some of them running, others shaking their heads desperately, and all wending their way upwards. From every nook and wash-out the great slopes disgorged them, herd following herd till they united on the beaten deer paths. There was much disagreement and grunting and shaking of velvet horns, but it was noticeable that, as usual, the hinds led and the stags followed. Corrie and Greyface moved upwards with the rest.

Reaching a high plateau their own herd spread out, or rather it began to disintegrate into separate herds, and it was here that Greyface and Corrie fell in with the grey hinds Greyface had marshalled by the ruined clachan. Here was the sleek old grandma with the well-groomed coat, here also the hind calf of Corrie's age with the white star upon her forehead. If the stag calf remembered them at all, he was certainly not particularly interested in them, and would have gone on but that Greyface chose to dally. The old stag passed from hind to hind licking their faces, and when the sleek old hind led on, Greyface fell in at the tail-end of the herd, which is the accustomed place for a king stag when the herd is on the move. Only when exceptional boldness is required does a stag move to the fore; normally he covers the rear, for it is from that direction the wolf danger would normally have come.

The hinds had not yet dropped their calves, but were on their way to the high tablelands to do so. The terrace on which they had met was half-way up the Mam Shiel, and now the old hind led the way to the deer path which ran across the face of the cliff, with three hundred feet to the screes below. It was not the safest way, though certainly the shortest, and driven from their lower shelter some of the hinds were anxious to reach their calving haunts.

Strung out after the old hind were her daughters, several of them still accompanied by their last year's calves, each calf in front of its mother so that where the way was difficult it had its mother's nose to nudge it and help it on; but at the tail-end of the line a stag calf wearing a red collar followed at the heels of his lord and master, with no one to help him should the need arise.

It was a perilous pathway with the treacherous cliff falling away almost sheer on their left and rising vertically on their right, in places no more than stepping-stones and no wider than a deer's body. Here and there the track had been washed away for a yard or two, leaving gaps of wet peat and stones apt to yield underfoot. Over these the deer had to jump or scramble as best they could, yet judging from the giddy places to which they habitually climb they were perfectly capable of it.

Scarcely was the train of deer strung out along the pathway than His Majesty the eagle appeared overhead. He was circling very high but obviously keeping an eye on the herd lest misfortune befall them. The old hind leading paused a fraction of a second and looked up at him. In the clear light she could see his bright eyes and his separate tail and flight feathers as he wheeled slowly. She had not bargained for his company, but it was now too late to turn back. If she did so the whole line would telescope, and all would have to turn on the narrow foothold. It is against the law of the shelves to turn back, for not only does it cause confusion, but it may start temporary panic among those uncertain of the danger ahead. Therefore, she slightly quickened her pace, and Corrie at the end of the procession felt very much alone.

Yet he had the familiar hindquarters of Greyface to lead him, and how very familiar they must have been! The high, dark-maned shoulders, the broad neck, the light disc of his stern quarters with the black diamond of his tail set in the center of it. Where Greyface led, Corrie had confidence to follow.

Ahead of Greyface was one of those treacherous gaps where the path had subsided. It afforded no safe foothold, and was perhaps four feet across. Greyface took it in his stride, and the eagle circled lower. One could see the golden sheen of his plumage as he banked in the sunbeams, and he was watching the calf at the end of the line, for that was irregular. If the calf jumped too soon the stag ahead would block the way, and that might mean disaster.

Corrie made no mistake. He waited till Greyface was well ahead before he nerved himself to jump, but the eagle saw his chance. Down he came like a thunderbolt, meaning to catch the calf in mid-leap, striking at his face. His flight feathers screamed as he checked himself, for Corrie had balked at the last moment. He had stopped and drawn back at the moment of leaping, and now he was on his hind-legs ready to ward off the blow with his fore-hoofs. It was a clever move on his part, as though he had known the eagle's intention.

The blast from the bird's wings beat up an eddy of dust. He stopped in mid-air and seemed to drop tail first. He passed from view, for from the track no one could see the screes, so far away were they and so steep the cliff. But the white bones of deer were collected there.

It is generally thought that old stags play no intimate part in the defense of their young. They leave that to the hinds, but more than once a stag has been seen to shepherd a calf out of danger, and that was what Greyface did now. As the scream of wings stabbed the quietude Greyface pivoted round where one would have thought there was scarcely foothold for a cat, so that for a moment he and Corrie were face to face. Corrie saw the move, and he, too, turned to make room for Greyface. And in a moment the big stag was back across the gap, the calf under his fore-hoofs, under his extended neck, and in this manner they went back without haste.

Meantime the hinds went steadily on, without faltering, without looking back.

※ ※ ※

CHAPTER 6

Corrie and Greyface continued their climb sky-
wards by a different route, and they saw no more
of the grey-faced hinds till on the following day
they gained the tablelands. This was the world
of the mountain tops, the realms of the dotterel
and the ptarmigan, with only the sky overhead
and the stony wastes stretching on all sides. It
was a world of supreme peace except when the
winds blew ten thousand devils (which they did
pretty constantly), a world frequently shut off by
an ocean of clouds from the gloom below, where

man crawled and had his being. Moonlight or sun, these clouds were often a fairyland of color, stretching on all sides more vast than the ocean as man generally looks upon it, and at this season the sun was glaring in its intensity. There were no troublesome insects, though those which lived on honey existed in a variety of gauzy winged forms, darting between the clumps of saxifrages that clung with tough roots to the stony ground. Some of these, too, were exquisitely colored, as were the luxuriant clumps of moss which sent a shimmer of delicate hues over the whole land-scape, particularly at dawn and sunset.

Here the hinds would nurse their newly born calves—some, indeed, had already arrived—and as they lay among the plants and stones their mottled coats afforded such perfect harmony that a man might have stepped upon them. There were many hinds, and since the different clans lived separately their distinctions were very marked. One saw the same family likeness running from hind to hind in one herd. Some of them were very red, others yellow, others lighter in shade, almost grey like Greyface and Corrie and the grey hinds with whom Greyface had run. Some had long faces and donkey ears; others were broader-headed

and more compact in build, and one accustomed
to their faces would have seen as much variety
among them as among human beings. The easygoing, the spiteful, the vain, the shrewd, the
garrulous, all were there, but to every herd there
was the beloved grandma with the well-groomed
coat whom the others were constantly licking.

Though they accompanied the herd of grey
hinds, Corrie and Greyface did not associate with
them for the first few days, and Corrie, accom-
panying his old partner, would somewhat wist-
fully watch the rollicking games of the calves of
his own age as they galloped hither and thither,
lightly as gale-borne thistle seed. Often the little
hind with the white star on her forehead would
stand and stare at him rather rudely, and one
evening she went up to him and began to butt
him about. Corrie was at first a little embarrassed
and tried to keep out of her way, but she insisted
till he had to return butt for butt, and before he
knew it they were playing. And as they played,
the flowers about them changed from purple to
scarlet, from scarlet to mauve, then the whole
stony desert surrounding them assumed the color
of soft gold, and the calves themselves became
little figures of bronze.

Thus opened up a new and a happier phase of Corrie's life; for, from playing alone with Starpoint, it was not long before he was dragged into the games of the other calves, and here was an exact repetition of the games he had played in the castle grounds, save that the parts he had never understood were simplified. The same Hide-and-Seek, the same imaginary cat hunts, the same King-of-the-Castle, for some of the stag calves had their own terraces on which they resented the trespass of others.

But in spite of his newly found merriment Corrie did not neglect his old friend. At intervals between the games he would look up suddenly as though he had forgotten something, then he would go over to Greyface to assure himself that all went well with him. Sometimes Starpoint would go with him and sniff the old stag's nostrils, at which he would nose her away impatiently in a way that indicated that he had no use for hind calves. Starpoint would resent that. With head lowered she would try to butt his legs from under him, but Greyface, hardly aware of her buffetings, would go on nosing among the Alpine plants, paying no heed to such impudence.

I believe that Greyface and Corrie loved each

other very dearly, but not in the way father and son love each other in our own world, and not as Corrie would have loved his mother who could never have gained these hinterlands. A sense of retrospect plays little part in the lives of wild animals, save that they profit by experience; prospect plays a still smaller part. Tomorrow and yesterday hardly figure in their affections, yet one can miss the other very sorely, and neither will rest so long as they are apart. But given each other's company, each goes its own way, at times utterly regardless of the other's welfare. In their world each individual must guard its own interests.

The year-old calves were an independent, self-willed lot, but as the new calves grew they began to form sports committees of their own. At present their one idea of playing was to scamper up and down, up and down, with no idea of adding to their own or to each other's merriment, and the faintest unfamiliar sound or breath of wind would send them scampering back to their mothers. There was one little fellow among them who had no mother, or rather had several mothers. He was a week or two older than the rest of the newly born, and probably he had come into the world on the lower slopes, and his young mother had died at his birth. He loved to play with the older calves of Corrie's ilk, but they were far too fast for him, and soon he would find himself stranded alone in the vast desert of stones. At that he would run to the nearest adult he saw, and sometimes it was Greyface, who would lick his face and then ignore him. It seemed that any one of the grey-faced hinds would feed him when he persisted, but he quickly became independent of them. He was a hardy and courageous little fellow.

Corrie's red collar was becoming somewhat ragged about the edges, for the other calves were forever nibbling and pulling at it. It is conceivable that they envied him this adornment, and would have loved to possess red collars of their own. And so the pleasant days of early summer drifted by— just drifted in a succession of fairy dawns and sunsets.

As the little calves grew their mothers appeared to become tired of constantly watching over them, or perhaps it was that as their demands on their mothers grew it became necessary for the hinds to travel farther afield to find food. This was a sparse land and the deer had to graze a larger area than would have been necessary in the sheltered corries where there is food on all sides. Up here it was strong and nourishing, but they had to travel farther for it, and so the nursing hinds formed the habit of taking their children to Grandma at an appropriate hour. Then Grandma would lie on her appointed knoll, placidly chewing the cud, while the little company of infants surrounding her gradually grew. As each hind brought her calf she would nudge it down in the nursery circle, bidding it stay with Grandma, then all the young hinds would go gadding off in glorious freedom.

So in the early forenoon Grandma would find herself completely surrounded by a bevy of mottled youngsters who perfectly well understood that they were in her care. She was not fussy about them, but she liked to know exactly where they were. On the whole they were very good and obedient, for this was their rest time, but if the one-year-olds came running up with a rumble of hoofs, half the infants would get up for a scamper with them. They were soon left behind, and there they would stand one by one, uttering the piercing calf cry, at which Grannie would stand up on her knoll so that they could see her, and go back. And when they had all returned Grannie would go her round, sniffing each in turn.

One morning the wind suddenly got up and the plateau was swept by a sandstorm. There was no shelter up here, so the hinds lay down with their backs to the wind and their calves sheltered under them. Soon the gale threatened to sweep them off the plateau, and an old hind rose, leading the way to the brink of the plateau. The other hinds fell in behind her, and behind the herd came Greyface savagely driving them forward.

Greyface gave no quarter. He simply slashed and pounded the hinds ahead of him, driving them over the edge, and whipping in any other hinds which chanced to cross his path. He drove them clean off the tablelands, and soon an immense herd of hinds and calves, with not a few young stags of all denominations, were fleeing at the heels of the old grey-faced hind. She led them down the defiles to the very brink of the Corrie Rou, where the great herd split up into smaller herds, all filing downwards to the more sheltered levels. Less than an hour later cakes of ice the size of dinner plates were crashing down on the tablelands, and even in the sheltered hollows many young calves were pelted to death by the hailstones.

Looking down the caldron of the Corrie Rou from the foot of the semi-circular cliffs was like looking down a closed-in valley, the slopes of which appeared almost vertical. Far below the valley suddenly ceased, for here it opened out on the mountain face with the big swamp and the river beyond it. The right-hand side of the caldron was green, for it caught the sun, but the opposite side was accumulated screes from the skyline to the bottom, rocks of all shapes and sizes lying on top of each other, some the size of a church. Therefore the deer used only the sunny side, and through time they had trampled out deep roadways which ran parallel along its entire face. It was along one of these pathways that the old hind led the grey-faced herd, often sheltering under the cliff from the storm, but nearing the end of the caldron she suddenly left the main path, crossed the boulder-strewn bottomlands of the caldron by a scarcely definable path, then mounted sharply to the mouth of another valley which ran off at right angles into a little isolated and forgotten world. Only the oldest resident deer appeared to know of this screened offshoot from the Corrie Rou, but so vast was the whole area that there was room for a dozen little valleys to pass unnoticed.

The little valley was a cul-de-sac, for the end of it was closed by a vertical cliff like the Corrie Rou itself. It was filled with scrub oak and hazel, scarcely more than a half a mile in width, its sides very steep so that it afforded perfect shelter from storms. The old hind might have known this, for that August was memorable for its hailstorms, which deer hate because hail stings their ears.

There were no other deer in the little valley of the hazels when the herd arrived, and for the calves it was a perfect playground into which the sun streamed continuously. They could hide behind the trees and run in and out among the bushes, but the year-olds had scarcely become established when they met the rightful owner—a little roebuck who lived there with his wife and their fawn. Though no bigger than the youngest calf he could, I veritably believe, have turned the red deer out, for he was as quick as a weasel and his small upright horns were deadly stabbing weapons. Clearly he resented the intrusion, and

at once he proceeded to make this fact known—
mainly by attacking Corrie.

Corrie's red collar must have been the cause of
it, for only in that was he different from the other
calves. At all events the buck soon made the
young stag's life a nightmare of watchfulness, for
in the middle of their games a red streak would
suddenly appear in the midst of them. He was
come and gone like a flash, but meantime Corrie
would have to leap for his life to avoid those
dagger horns. The little buck was savagely intent,
and even Greyface could have done nothing in the
matter, had he indeed been sufficiently interested.

Though there were always herds of deer scattered among the terraces on the green slopes of
Corrie Rou, hinds with young calves rarely harbored there, for in addition to the nesting eagles
it was an impregnable stronghold of foxes and
wildcats, occupying the cairns once held by bear
and wolf. It is not wise to make one's home next
to the dens of thieves, even though one may be
well armed against them. So far as could be judged
the valley of the hazels was reasonably free from
such vermin, yet late one evening the agonized
screaming of the roe-deer fawn brought the herd
of red deer smartly to attention. The cry came

from the rocky slope immediately above where they were resting, and instantly every hind set off in that direction, snorting defensively.

They had not gone far when a bundle of bristling and brindled fur came rolling down to meet them. It was a wildcat embracing the roe-deer fawn, her strong paws entwined about his neck and her terrible fangs at work behind his ears. As her terrified prey struck out she was cleverly using the impulses of his hind-legs to keep them rolling, for that was the easiest way to avoid the stabbing hoofs of the fawn's parents.

A small tiger she was, or something worse than a tiger for her size—forty-two inches from tip to tip. She was merely hanging on to the struggling fawn till such time as she could shift her grip to his throat, after which, having made sure of him, she would dart into the branches or the screes, glad enough to leave him to his parents till later, when she might return.

But the interception of the red deer upset her plans, for they were all round her in a moment. She shot off, and with a hissing snarl made for the nearest tree trunk, which unfortunately for her was broken off seven feet from the ground.

Still she reached the top, and crouched there, her broad ears laid back, her green eyes blazing furiously. Nowhere in the world could one have found a more complete picture of feline spite.

Corrie was with the herd, and in his eyes one might have seen the same dare-devil gleam as when he and Chang hunted the village cats together. At all events he knew, or thought he knew, a great deal about their gigantic gift for bluff, and he was not to be so easily bluffed. Frequently he had left Chang to do the baiting while he went quietly in from the other side, and this appeared a favorable opportunity for such tactics.

In their anger the hinds had no more sense than to gather round the head end of the cat, and she was cleverly holding them there by pouring the liquid fire of her tongue into their faces. Thus she would have held them until they were blind with fury, when she would have a chance to turn about and make for safer cover. But Corrie's chance came sooner. He slipped round to the other side of the stump, where the blunt black tip of her tail was curling ominously. There he made a terrific sky-hop, and his fore-hoofs struck the bristling body with a force that precipitated her head foremost straight into the faces of the assembled hinds.

Probably no one but Corrie knew how it happened, and the hinds did not all get off unscathed, for the cat broke her fall by clinging to the face of the one immediately below, and then she got her fangs and her terrible hind legs to work. Another second and Starpoint's mother would have lost her eyes, but a second is a long time in such a rough-and-tumble, and Greyface did a thing one would hardly have expected of a stag. In an instant he had his teeth round the cat's neck, and had torn her loose. As she fell, one of his hoofs went down in a deadly stab, completely disabling her.

The hinds finished it, all but the hind whose face was streaming blood. She had experienced enough and quietly crept away. But the others were thick on the spot, jostling each other for a place in the melee, and their hoofs thundered down.

Nor was the roebuck absent. He had slipped in under them and was raining down blows with the rest, only his hindquarters visible in the general scrimmage. But Corrie recognized them, and he got in a double-fisted blow which knocked the roebuck clean out of the fight, without his even knowing who had hit him. Nor did they ever see him again, or his doe and her fawn, so they must have gone clear away from the valley of the hazels.

That night the hinds slept in a ring with their calves in the center, no doubt all dreaming their wildcat dreams, for deer are great dreamers. Grey-face was restless and ill at ease, and several times during the dark hours he prowled round the ring, sniffing the faces of the hinds for assurance that all went well with them.

Red deer are not devoid of bravery, but they believe in avoiding trouble rather than facing it. Being mobile, they will at once leave a place where trouble has occurred, and go right away rather than risk a repetition. So at daybreak they quietly filed out of the little valley of the hazels and returned to the caldron. They had left the wildcat no more than a pulp trodden into the hard earth, but wildcats have been known to hunt in pairs, particularly when there are "kits" to feed.

The herd grazed quietly across the green slopes below Corrie Rou till the sun was well up; later they drifted towards the mouth of the caldron overlooking the fertile glen. Evidently they meant to graze slowly down to the lower levels, and by evening they would probably have finished up in the big swamp had not something unforeseen happened. It took the form of the bark of a rifle not very far away, and upon Greyface the effect was electrical. He froze, exactly where he stood, and for fully a minute remained absolutely still, searching the slopes below, while Corrie went up to him and also searched.

Greyface must have seen something, for suddenly he broke off straight down the incline at a brisk trot. He left the hinds without a single thought or a backward glance, and Corrie also left them, but with many lingering backward glances, for he was leaving Starpoint, his playmate, and she was gazing after him. Yet unwaveringly he followed Greyface, though he did not understand— he did not understand! He knew only that there was deadly peril, for Greyface was afraid—more terribly afraid than ever before during their friendship. About rifle fire Corrie knew nothing at all, but perhaps he could guess a good deal, and there can be no doubt that he associated it all with the rifle shot. It was, indeed, as well that Greyface should leave the hinds.

Never before had Greyface behaved like this. He seemed bewildered and undecided which way to go, and no sooner had they started off in one direction than he seemed to see danger ahead and turn aside to take another route. From his conduct one might have thought that a ghost army of armed men was hidden about the moor, yet they heard no more rifle fire.

They were making for the lower woods, but it seemed that they would never get there, and all the time Greyface was warning—"Keep down! Keep down or they will see us!" Corrie knew that it was man they had to fear, man whom he had always trusted and would have trusted now in the castle grounds, though here man was a different creature—a deadly enemy. Greyface and all the wild deer had repeatedly made this plain.

They reached the woods at length, but they struck a young planting which was newly fenced and there was no way through the high barrier. In vain Greyface rammed it with his horns, striving to force a way through, till in despair he turned into the old heather and lay down, flat as a calf in a deep thicket, while Corrie watched from the bank above. But not a human soul did he see. Everything was peaceful, and a herd of switches and knobbers were grazing idly not far off. They would not have remained there had there been any danger.

When dusk descended it was Corrie who led the way, down by steep pathways till they came to the river. They crossed by the white stone to the twisted alders on the other side, where once they had slept and dreamed. They did not dally there. The lights of the village were still twinkling, but they followed strips of woodland till, by ways known only to Corrie, they reached the bracken field. Hiding from the terrors of man they had yet sought his very haunts, but there was no feed of hay for them tonight. They waited till the village was dark and silent, and then, turning back, passed high above to where the woods were sanctuary. There any deer could harbor, for it was a rule of the forest that there was no shooting on this side. Not far from the village a long strip of woodland ran down the valley. It was a very old forest, mainly of spruce trees towering to the sky, but it was divided in two, each half having its own name. The village end where the road bordered it was known for a mile as the Singing Forest, for many of the old trees leaned against their neighbors, and when there was any wind their entwined branches, rubbing together, gave forth a constant singing.

So when the wind began to blow the whole great wood would strike up its orchestra, and it was said that foxes would not stay there, because they distrusted the many strange voices.

But long ago heather fire had entered the wood from the other end, where the old heather and blueberry bushes under the trees grew to a man's height. The fire had left the great trees practically untouched, but it had burnt deeply into the peat and destroyed the roots of many of them. They had taken several years to die, and many still stood, stark and barkless. This was the Dead Forest, and so the old wood stands to this day, one half of it dead and the other half still living, the living the Singing Forest, the dead the Dead Forest.

It was impossible to gain the Singing Forest from the roadway end on account of the deer fence, so the two deer went on down the valley till they came to a wide gap in the fence which the foresters had opened up for timber haulage, and by this gap they entered the Dead Forest.

All this region Corrie knew, for he had explored it at night time ere he finally left man's threshold. To him the great forest had always been a beloved haven, and it was to remain so all his days.

Never had the two deer been aware of such a

sense of repose and security as they felt in the retreat of the great wood while they strayed. Here the big trees were thinly scattered, but under them the old heather rose above their shoulders, and on all sides the ground was scattered with fallen trees and their interlaced branches, forming a barrier through which they had to pick their way. No gale would have reached them in the shelter they sought that night, lying close together, for there was no need for Corrie to mount a high point from which to watch. They were no longer master and attendant, but two close friends living in each other's companionship, and after a long, lingering twilight, when night began to creep through the wood like a great and gracious presence, they watched a company of grey crows assembling to roost in the fork of two tall spruces which leaned affectionately against each other. They alighted silently, grey-cloaked little figures more like goblin residents of the silent place than things of blood and feathers, but having assembled they were not for long silent. While the skies were still aflame one took the center of the ring, and spreading his wings at intervals, held forth at length in guttural tones, his strange voice seeming to emphasize rather than break the silence.

When he had finished and had duly been applauded another took his place, and so on till it grew quite dark, when their voices slowly subsided into the quietude. No doubt they were discussing their fortunes during the day, for the grey crows scour the country in families, and only at their recognized roosting places do they unite. Scoundrels they may be, yet like all crows they stand high in their family lives, and their quiet voices seemed to add to the peace and sanctuary of the big wood.

The stag's great horns had now dried out, but they were still draped with untidy ribbons of velvet which flapped before his eyes and certainly added nothing to his grace and dignity. While he and Corrie rested in the wood he was constantly rubbing his horns against convenient branches and thrashing at the thorny undergrowth with them. In this way he got rid of the untidy ribbons and soon he was what is known as a "clean" stag, regarded by man as fit for any hunter's prowess. He was probably at that time the finest head on the range, for even Royals are rare and Imperials improbable in any forest where there is no woodland feeding. Greyface had been known for some years now as an outlying stag, and such beasts somehow escape the eye of the stalker watching over them, till their prime is past and they have served their useful purpose. It is then as well that the ground should be cleared of them, for there can be no doubt that young beasts father the best calves.

That is the normal course of survival. Through past ages the wolf and the bear have kept the herds fit by killing off the weak and the aged, so that only the fittest breed their kind, and since such enemies are now gone, man himself must do the weeding out designed to keep the herds up to standard. It is similarly as well that old hinds should not be left to litter up the terraces, but here judgment should be liberally mingled with mercy. Old and unfertile hinds often play an important part in the welfare of herd life, as we have seen in the case of Grandma. They lead their daughters by the safest roads and know what ails the herd when they lose their brightness of coat and luster of eye. It is then that the old hind leads the herd to the seashore where they can obtain the salt and iodine they need—or perhaps to a recess of the mountains where a certain herb grows which will soon restore their fitness. Holding the secrets of the past and handing them on, weather-wise and familiar with the safest paths, these old hinds inspire confidence in the herds, so that while winter hind-shooting is favorable to the larder, it is as well that it falls mainly to the stalkers and gillies, who at least know the herds.

Though the brambles and the blueberries were now ripe and the tinker families had come to pick them, there was room enough in the big wood, and the deer were not disturbed by these gypsy people there in their own interests. For over a week they dallied about the sunny aisles, putting on weight for the lean months ahead, but the roaring season was drawing near, and Greyface was becoming more and more restless. Well might they have remained there till the following spring, with food and abundance on all sides, following the roe-deer pathways to the sweetest feeding grounds with never a care in the world, but when the urge came Greyface had to go. Corrie was reluctant, remembering the strange fear which the world without was holding, but of course he followed Greyface. They went at nighttime, down the glen to cross the river by the white stone, then up the mountain face towards the heights of the great corrie.

It was a perfect September daybreak when they settled to rest on the stony slope high above the big swamp. In the far distance they could see the long strip of woodland in which they had harbored, a shimmer of blue across the valley, and here and there a cornfield waved golden in the soft breeze of morning. Corrie as usual lay a few yards higher up the slope than Greyface, and both of them were completely at peace. They watched a fox daintily picking his way between the peat pools on the swamp below, a minute speck human eyes would never have noticed, while overhead a family of buzzards circled, their thin-edged mewing floating softly down.

Yet there was something strange about that morning, an unfamiliar atmosphere of which the deer were subtly conscious, and though the sky was cloudless, like a thousand thousand dawns on the great Corrie Rou, the sun was no sooner well up than it began to get dark. It was not the darkness of an approaching storm, for it was the same on all sides like a great shadow upon the land, in the company of which no other shadows could exist. Old Sol was still riding high in the bluest of deep-blue skies, yet he seemed to cast no light, and night was steadily descending. Birds ceased to sing, and in the unearthly twilight Corrie rose uneasily and began to scrutinize the slopes. Had he looked at the sun he would have seen it in the form of a crescent which was steadily narrowing, till soon it hung like a fiery new moon, then darkness settled.

Darkness three hours after dawn and a cloudless sky! Silence reigned everywhere, and the earth seemed reluctant to release the sunshine it so recently held, for a pale effulgence hung everywhere and the hollows were no darker than the ridges. Somewhere a stoat struck up his sharp flint-like "chipp-chipp-chipp" till it seemed to fill the whole still air, though it was but a small sound. Presently they saw his white front as he sat bolt upright among the stones, his black-tipped tail jerking vertically with each fresh outburst. The earth began to give off its fragrance as it does when night gathers, and the burnt hillside had assumed the same blue as the skies, though the stones remained chalky white.

High overhead there sounded the harsh notes of a peregrine descending from the Corrie Rou. He came down the mountain face in one prodigious dive, spinning wing over wing as he fell with the scream of a descending shell. He passed low over the heads of the two deer, and Corrie dipped his ears, then still revolving was half across the swamp ere he flattened out and bounded heavenwards.

Presently there came another twinkle of sunshine like the first ray of dawn, then slowly the light improved in the same progressive way as it had faded. The eclipse was over, and quickly the old world was returning to normal. Greyface rose and stretched himself, and from high above there sounded that same short, sharp report that had struck such terror to the heart of Greyface a week ago.

It was not a terrifying sound, for it was softened by the teeth of a silencer: far more terrifying was the shriek of the bullet and the deadly thud of impact. The bullet went burling on to cast up a volcano of peat slush in the swamp far below, and the velocity of it was frightful. It seemed veritably to pass between Corrie's ears, and Greyface, just beyond, did not know what had happened to him. For some seconds he stood stock-still, then he turned and set off down the hillside.

Neither did Corrie know what had befallen his comrade, and he never would know. Nothing short of fire will turn a breaking deer, and even fire would not have stayed the headlong plunge of the old Imperial. Faster and faster he fled, the loose stones clicking under his flying hoofs, till he fell and rose, and fell again.

Corrie tried to follow, but there was no keeping pace with the final race of the stricken stag. Smaller and smaller Greyface became as the distance between them increased, Greyface heedless of that short, shrill calf cry, the first time Corrie had ever uttered it in entreaty to him. He saw Greyface leave the edge of the cliff that falls sheer to the swamp, and there remained only the branches of the rowan tree clinging to the brink of it, for Greyface was gone.

Instantly Corrie knew that it was too late to call now, yet he followed faithfully to the end. He peered over the edge of the cliff and saw Greyface swinging below, caught by his horns in the branches of the rowan. So he would continue to swing till the storms and the ravens left his white bones to clatter in the wind, till even they were gone, and only his splendid antlers remained inexorably held in the fork of the mountain ash.

❧ ❧ ❧

CHAPTER 7

Corrie remained there, looking down, till he heard voices descending the slope, whereupon he stole off and hid among the screes. The laird and Callum looked down, and Callum shook his head dolefully. "It's a pity, sir, but we may as well leave him there," he said. "He's smashed to bits and both his horns are broken."

Just then there sounded the sharp bleat of a calf close at hand and, turning, they saw Corrie coming to them, Corrie wearing his battered red collar, calling repeatedly as he ran to them, seeking their aid in his dilemma. He looked very small and very much a calf, though several months had elapsed since last he felt the caress of human fingers. He went straight to Callum, and the three of them looked down at the great Greyface.

The laird turned away impulsively. His eyes were upon the ground and he spoke with a strange huskiness. "Fiona's pet," he said. "Come away, Callum. Nothing can be gained by standing here."

Callum nudged Corrie aside, and they began to mount the hill. At the place where Greyface was struck they paused and looked back. There was blood on the stones at their feet, and blood leading down the slope to the edge of the cliff where the stag calf still stood, looking down.

"That, according to reports, is Corrie's father," observed the laird. "Callum, I'm finished stalking! I've had too many years at it already. Your father and I will pack up together. You can take over Master Alastaire next autumn."

But Callum merely shook his head. "Nothing of the kind, sir," said he. "Who ever heard of one of the finest shots in the country giving up because of a wee bit stag calf? Yon old stag was past his prime, and it was time he went whatever."

But that night the laird cleaned and oiled his rifle and hung it on two hooks in the gun cupboard. On a shield opposite hung a short dagger on its green shield, beautifully engraved and set

with Cairngorm stones, and on its ebony handle
were inscribed the words:

*"Behold my sghean-dubh! Sharpened and crys-
talized and keen as steel, understanding comes to
me this day that never again will I raise my hand
to kill."*

Chuckling grimly the laird hung the dagger
beside his rifle for Callum to see.

Till darkness fell, Corrie remained with his old
companion, then he went to look for him else-
where. He must have known that the long trek
at the old stag's heels was now at an end, yet
with the restlessness of a dog that has lost its
master he went to look for him in all the places
where he was accustomed to seeing him. Their
last few days together had been very pleasant,
and though Corrie knew that Greyface was gone
he could not help looking for him because of the
empty loneliness which possessed him. How he
reconciled Callum's appearance with the death of
his chum we cannot understand. Did he know
now that man who gives so liberally with one
hand is ever ready to take with the other? Did
he realize that not the eagle, nor thunder, nor the
wildcat were his real foes? That withal man was

outstanding among them and always would be? Certain it was that at last he understood the deadly meaning of rifle fire, and would always fear it, though in his old friend Callum he could not have recognized the true killer, or he would not have gone to him so fearlessly at the time of his loss.

During the next few days he wore himself to a shadow looking for Greyface. He crossed the river by the white stone and wandered restlessly about the Dead Forest by the roe-deer pathways. He turned back and searched the rocky hinterland; down to Corrie Rou and along the length of the little valley of the hazels, where he found the foul remains of the wildcat. Many scores of miles he must have searched till hope died and he forgot what he was looking for. He had perhaps forgotten Greyface in the material sense, yet the sense of loss remained.

So he stood on the mountainside one starlight night at the mouth of the great Corrie and looked down upon the glen. There was the little loch with its many islands, set like a jewel among the Green Braes, and far in the distance the lights of what had once been his home. He thought he could hear the grunting of hinds somewhere across the great grey loneliness, and he called once—that thin stab of sound which a calf utters when it is alone. From down the mountain face came an answer, and madly in that direction he ran, calling and listening repeatedly, and every time, drawing nearer, an answer came.

At length he saw her, a little grey outline in the starlight. He could even see the white star upon her forehead, and they ran eagerly together to caress each other's face.

She took him back to the grey hinds, who gathered round him and sniffed him from end to end to make sure that no hurt had come to him. There had been rifle fire on the hills for many days, and they knew that Greyface was dead. Perhaps they spoke of his wisdom and how great he had been among his kind, gentle with his hinds and anxious for their welfare at all seasons, for that is a great trait to be found only in an occasional King stag. A King he had been, and he was the father of Corrie, as yet too young to show how he would mature.

But later the darkening of a stormy night again brought round the bugling of stags. The grey hinds were high up on the terraces of the Corrie Rou, and clear and wild and melancholy the chaotic music rang, stag answering stag from the terraces and the gullies and the ridges. So the orchestra struck up once more and another season of activity began——a mad stampede of activity, to crowd into a few days all that had to be made up for ten months of inaction by storm and sunshine. Another night and the affrighted atmosphere was torn from the Cairngorms to beyond Ben-y-Gloe and throughout Rannoch and the endless hinterlands of the Grampians.

The big stags did not come in herds but as individuals, challenging each other, trying to outflank each other, hating each other. One might have thought that the world had moved back into the incomprehensible recesses of time when terrible creatures haunted the valleys, and man himself had to seek the mountain-tops to escape the maw of his foes. They swept the terraces of Corrie Rou before them, an invading army, but an army of lust and greed, having no discipline, no organized purpose. A hundred prisoners might be taken by midnight, and as many would escape before dawn. The fortunes of the season were as yet in the melting-pot; they were there to possess, but too eager and greedy to hold what they won. Only an occasional big greyface lower down had as yet established a herd and held a terrace. The predominating horde of yellow stags from behind the Corrie Rou were as yet a rabble, sweeping madly over the ridges with deadly jealousy for each other.

Plunging down to the terrace where the grey hinds were harbored came such a stag. One might have thought he was a messenger of death, so grim and forbidding he looked, his head thrown back, his coarse hair clogged with peat slush, and roaring constantly as he bore down upon them. Away to the left descended another stag, a ten-pointer in his prime, for though light he was perfectly proportioned. Now they challenged each other till above the clamor of echoes the night air shook.

The calves of Corrie's year hunched together as both stags broke into a gallop towards them, descending the rocky slope at reckless speed. In the darkness stones came clattering down from under their pounding hoofs, the thunder of which grew and faded. The old stag reached the hinds first and tried to herd them, but they fanned out as they ran, and the ten-pointer, the swifter of the two, cleverly cut in and slashed half the parcel of hinds over to his side.

It was a fair division, for each stag was now

racing down the middle, parallel if not quite flank to flank, each rumbling defiance, each with his flustered hinds running parallel on the other flank, and so the space between them would steadily have widened but that the bunch of stampeding calves was racing straight in front of them.

The ten-pointer quickened his speed till a crash seemed inevitable. His slender legs must surely go on the broken foothold, for he seemed to be clearing thirty yards at a bound on the almost vertical descent. The stones clicked and flew and in a few seconds he had overtaken the herd of flustered calves, and slashing with his antlers set them racing to the right straight into the herd of his angry rival. It was a very pretty piece of Spartan irony, for he might have said, "Here you are, Milord. You can take charge of the children!"

But these early conquests were all to no purpose, for other stags were sweeping the corrie downwards, so that in the caldron's depths all the wives were pooled, and it was not even a case of the winner taking the pool. Stags were careering and roaring in all directions, cutting in and warding off, while the hinds, in groups, merely trotted sedately where they wanted to go, so that a herd of two hundred deer pouring over the caldron's edge would spread by their own selected runways over the lower mountain face. And the season would go on till it lost its madness, and the real King stags had collected their herds and were able, to some extent, to hold them.

For the calves it was a harrowing time. Most of them had lost their herds, though a few managed to cling together, and as that first night wore on, the bleating of the season's youngsters could be heard on all sides. Many of their mothers, whirled into the merry-go-round, did not care, for their calves were really independent of them. By no means were the hinds beaten and driven; on the contrary, they were complete mistresses of the situation; for they had merely to run and a dozen stags would career after them, and they could slip away as they passed from knoll to knoll and desert each in turn.

As for the calves, no one wanted them, and by dawn Corrie had become one of a mixed rabble of youngsters scattered over the big swamp. Confusion was by then thrice confused, but in two days many of the big yellow stags had their herds collected. Along with other young stags Corrie would creep up through the bracken, but he lacked true determination and it never came to anything. Invariably he was driven out and had to flee for his life and some red-eyed monarch pounding behind him, till soon he lost interest in the whole affair, and with the colder weather he and other young beasts moved down towards the woods.

Slowly these youngsters gravitated into herds of their own and old friends drifted together. Starpoint was with Corrie and other calves of the greyface clan, even to the youngster of last spring who had lost his mother. There was still no rest in the forest, and it seemed one evening that Corrie was the only one among them who had somewhere to go, and because of that the others fell in behind him——seventeen calves in all.

They crossed the river by the white stone, and though it was at summer level owing to the long absence of heavy rains, the orphaned youngster clapped to the underside of Corrie, as he had crossed in the wake of Greyface, for Corrie was by far the strongest and sturdiest of the school of youngsters——probably the wisest, too, in view of his wide experiences. He led them quickly across the highway to the Dead Forest of pleasant memories, and they passed through the gap in the deer fence to melt away into the thickets.

Very happy they were there during the days that followed. The old heather took them into its folds and supreme peace descended upon the herd, which nevertheless resembled a band of lost and lonely children. The grey crows still assembled at dusk, and it is safe where the grey crows utter their good-night mutterings, while through the night their sentry would send forth his occasional "all's well" croak. The deer felt the safer for their watchfulness. They came to know the scurrying squirrels and the jay's call, for autumn was far spent and the sweet melancholy of it was uttered in the robin's song in the shadowy corners. But the dawns were still strangely devoid of dew, which at this season usually saturates the undergrowth, and still the rain held off.

On the fifth day the smell of smoke came down-wind through the Dead Forest. The big trees began to move till the earth also moved under their widespread tentacles. The wood became alive as the old trees sawed one against another, and withal—the smell of smoke!

At first the young deer paid little attention to it, for they were accustomed to the tang of smoke hanging low over the woods from the foresters' fires, but soon it began to thicken and the squirrels ran chattering along the pathways. Then fear began to dawn—the world-old fear of forest fire.

The infant was frightened and inclined to run off on his own, but always his confidence failed after a few bounds, and he returned to Corrie to paw at his forelegs and look up anxiously into his face. The other calves were gathered closely round, and Starpoint, too, was nudging Corrie. Yet he refused to be hustled and stood with ears up, gazing meditatively this way and that as Greyface might have done.

Soon they could hear the fire running up the trees and roaring through the undergrowth, rapidly approaching. The wind had increased in strength and the harsh voices of men came from the danger side. The fire fighters had arrived; it was time for the deer to move, and as though this dawned suddenly on Corrie's torpid mind he turned, high stepping, towards the Singing Forest. He should, of course, have made for the break in the deer fence for the open fields, but his instincts warned him to move downwind—the instincts that commanded his fathers before there were any deer fences or open fields; downwind they moved and into the darkness of the Singing Forest and the living trees.

The infant, beside whom Corrie looked enormous, was bounding at his side, and as they moved on through the thickets the smoke steadily thinned, and their fears subsided. Here the interlaced branches of the old conifers formed a dense canopy overhead, and they could only just hear the hush of the wind in their high spires. Yet the whole forest was moving, even to the sweet-scented pine-needles under their hoofs.

The air thickened again, and again they could hear the voices of the fire fighters, and the noise of the flames racing towards them. They had reached a cleared space under the trees where the branches had been trimmed back to a man's height, and there was a fireplace built of stones with one or two smoke-blackened tins propped against it. It was a recognized camping-place of the gypsies who had been there for the berry harvest, though they were now far gone on their road to the cities. Here the little herd stood bunched closely together, their big ears up, twitching their heads at every new sound, while the crackling grew to a roar which drowned the voices of the men and the swish of their fire beaters. The deer were as much afraid of the men as they were of the fire, for they did not know that the men were fighting to save the living trees from the holocaust descending upon them.

Suddenly there was a hot blast of wind, and the interlaced branches, dry as matchwood, took light twenty feet up from the ground. The deer saw a lane of fire racing towards them through the darkness, and they broke wildly, each one on its own, heedless of the rest. Crimson pathways of fire were now racing through the thickets in all directions, pouring liquid torrents of sparks on to the dry earth below. It lit up the darkest thickets, driving the herd of deer ahead of it towards the roadway—*and* the high deer fence.

Starpoint and the infant were following Corrie, for he knew the way. More than once in the castle days he had lain in the dense shadows of the wood and watched the ceaseless procession of holiday traffic passing along the road. It was fun to lie there in the darkness and security, seeing but unseen, fun to hear the voices of the people so near at hand as they passed blindly by. He knew that the deer fence was there, but had regarded it simply as a deer fence and had gone round instead of trying to force a way through. Now they must go through or die!

By the time they got there, there were roaring

lanes of fire on either side, and in the background a fitful glare. Without pausing they ran headlong into the deer fence, but only to be thrown back by it and to fall crumpled and half dazed into the undergrowth they had just left. They tried again, but clearly there was no way through, and on either side they could see their herd-mates similarly careering into the screen, while the fire behind them seemed to be forming an unbroken wall.

The infant had his head through the wire mesh and was struggling with all his strength to get through. As he fought his shrill cries of "Ma-Ma" rang above the din, that world-old cry which has rung down the ages, and sad it is when there is no mother to answer. Then two men came along the road on the other side of the deer fence. Their faces were blackened and streaked with sweat, while their clothing seemed to be hanging in ribbons like the antlers of Greyface when he and Corrie were here together. One of them Corrie should have known; the other was far older, though still a man of immense strength. It was the older man who croaked the words, "Drive them back, Callum, or they'll be grilled like rashers of bacon against the wire!" The younger man caught the infant by the ears, but could not drag him through. He took a pair of wire-cutters from his pocket and snapped the strands, then he tossed the youngster into the safety of the road-way. "Yon's a greyface!" he croaked to his companion.

Both of them fell to beating the fence with their birch-brooms to drive back the deer, and they went back, Starpoint following Corrie—back into the wall of fire. Some of them perished, but not all.

For a short space liquid fire seemed to be descending upon them from the hissing branches above, then they dashed out of it to find themselves close to the gypsy camp with burning lanes on all sides. They paused, undecided which way to go, as well they might be, till a roe-deer dashed up to them, doubled, then stampeded on. He had clearly been through the thick of it, for his coat was singed, his face almost naked; but there was nothing to show that he was blind. He stuck to his recognized pathway, dodging every obstacle, and where a roe leads it is wise to follow. So Corrie and Starpoint dashed after him, guided by his white hindquarters, and soon they were out of the heat and smoke and safely on the road to the open heather.

But Corrie had many times to wait for Star-point, looking back anxiously, for the shoulders of his beloved were burnt and she was suffering, while meantime the holiday-makers who had set the fire burning were well on their way to a distant city, their kettle and their picnic hamper neatly stowed away in its appointed place in the back of the car.

CHAPTER 8

Just before Christmas, snow fell on a frozen earth and, as in generations past, the village children took their sledges to the steep slope above the island where the deer crossed. The fun was at its height when they saw a great herd of deer passing over the skyline on the other side of the valley. The herd was already a mile long and moved in single file. Leading them was a big yellow-faced stag carrying a veritable eagle's nest of entangled deer-fence wire in his horns, for of late years many of the fences had sunk into disrepair, and rusty wire littered the edges of the plantings. Such wire presents a deadly danger to the red deer which, more than other animals, seem to possess the gift of getting into trouble of one kind or another. The hinds are apt to get their legs tied up in the wire and sometimes contrive to strangle themselves, while the stags gore at it in the rutting season till it becomes inexorably knotted and entangled in their antlers.

This was one of those local migrations which occur annually with the coming of hard weather. The snow had driven the deer down from the high country and they were in search of fresh feeding-grounds at the lower levels.

While normally it is the hinds who set the routine of the scattered herds, it is invariably a stag who moves to the fore when these mass movements occur. The old stag led by a hundred yards, then came a younger beast, a greyface, of about ten points. Another gap and then followed the general rabble of the herd, stags and hinds of all ages down to calves of last spring. It made a glorious picture in the frosty afternoon light, each beast clearly and sharply silhouetted against the rising land, so that in the stillness it almost seemed that one could hear the clicking of their many hoofs.

The big stag moved with an easy stride, apparently unhindered by the weight of wire in his horns. His head was thrown proudly back and his donkey ears flapped in time with his stride. Once he paused to glance towards the children, then he went heedlessly on as though unmindful of their proximity. His second-in-command occasionally glanced over his shoulder at those following, but he, too, seemed indifferent.

The line of deer already extended far up the valley, but still more were pouring over the skyline. It was thrilling to watch the ease and grace with which they took the high stone walls that separated the pastures, even the little calves scrambling over without the loss of a single second. The castle children ran home to tell their mother, and to warn Callum that there was likely to be a lively commotion at the top end of the valley tonight. Such a herd would strip the open grazing-lands like a swarm of locusts, and the tenant farmers could not be denied their winter venison. In this respect they regarded the deer in much the same light as the spawning salmon, firstly of value because they brought the wealthy to spend their money, secondly of value to them personally since they killed what they needed for larder and pickle keg. This they regarded as their inheritance.

From the battlements of the castle the herd was in full view, and the whole household assembled there. The tail end of the long line was now nearing the ridge, and far in the wake of the rest two small figures could be seen moving, hard put to it to keep up. They were a knobber and a hind calf of the same season.

The young stag was fit enough, but his companion was sorely smitten. Her neck was extended, her panting nostrils almost touching the trodden path. She was merely dragging one hoof after another, and clearly near the end of her strength. There was small wonder at this, for on her shoulders was an accumulated load of snow and ice, threatening to weigh her down in her tracks. Such things happen when a sick or starving beast becomes too weak to shake itself dry, for in this condition its coat loses its natural grease and its electricity, the one disability aggravating the other. Wounded stags are most commonly the victims.

But here was a sick hind, and the young stag was running round her anxiously watching the retreating herd. The wolf-fear was upon him, for through all time those who fall behind have been at the mercy of the following packs.

The young stag was very anxious. Repeatedly he went up to his companion, sniffing her ears, moving flank to flank with her as though to buoy up her hopes. So they reached a shallow washout down which a stream ran in wet weather, but it was now frozen solid. The stag bounded across and looked back for the hind to follow, but she would not attempt it, knowing it was far beyond her strength to mount the icy foothold on the other side. He went downstream a little way to an easier place, and gaily he led the way across, looking back for her to follow. Slowly she did so, but midway across she lost her foothold on the ice, and went down into the shallow water. The watchers could see at a glance that she had given up and would not attempt to rise; for all the terrors of earth and sky will not rouse a deer into making another kick in self-defense once its spirit is broken. The stag standing by was Corrie, the hind lying at his feet was Starpoint.

Alastaire closed his telescope with a click. "Come on, Fiona, come on, Callum," said he. "That hind's down for good. She's going to die in two inches of water. The young stag with her has a split ear."

Eagerly the three of them set out on their

mission of mercy. They left the household watching from the battlements, and it was the work of minutes only to harness the old horse to the sledge used for bringing shot hinds off the hill in winter.

But those on the rooftop were watching the continuation of the story. Scarcely was the young hind down than the leading stag seemed to sense something amiss in the wake of his herd. Hardly pausing in his stride he turned back, leaving the young greyface to carry on. As the two came face to face it seemed that some message passed between them, then back the yellowface went without another pause, wading deeply through the drift as he left the mass of the herd to the trodden pathway. He reached the end of the line and for a moment stood, still looking back by the way they had come. He could not see the two small figures far in the rear on account of the bank between them, but he seemed to know that they were there, for he went another hundred yards till they were in view. Then quickening his pace he went on towards them.

There was something set and determined in his stride now, something which forebode evil. Callum's young wife was the first to sense it: "My God, he's going to trample her!" she muttered.

The moments were tense, for there could be no doubt about it. For what other purpose could the old stag be returning so determinedly? Certainly not to help the young hind on her way. It was the fulfillment of the ancient law, that those who falter by the way must follow no farther. It is the weakest link that decides the strength of the chain.

As the yellowface neared the washout he broke into a canter which showed the supple strength of him. He was a big, bony beast, and his first act was to drive out the young stag and command him follow the trodden road. But Corrie stood by watching while the old stag went down to where Starpoint was lying. Still she did not try to rise.

Where were Callum and the children? They seemed to be taking an eternity in getting there, and the tension was now at breaking-point. The yellowface was standing over Starpoint, and they could see the grey breath bursting from his nostrils. The coarse hair of his shoulder-blades was on end, and he dealt her a vicious fore-hoof thrust, as if to tell her to rise. She extended her neck and seemed to shudder, a pitifully helpless little creature there in the snow.

The stag drew back and the women on the

battlements held their breath. They could almost see the murder in the big stag's eyes; and Corrie stepped desperately nearer. Then suddenly the stag paused, and the eagle's eyrie in his antlers rose into relief. He was looking towards the gate that led on to the moor. Callum was lifting it bodily from the drifts, and on the other side of it was the old horse and the strong sledge and the two children. A cheer went up from the battlements as the yellowface turned and went back without haste by the deeply trodden pathway of his herd.

There was a massacre of deer in the upper meadows that night, and among those that fell was an old stag whose horns were matted up with deer-fence wire. The crofter who shot him weighed them, and found that they held twenty-eight pounds of rusty wire. That was a big weight for a stag to carry.

The hind did not try to rise when Callum and the children went up to her. She merely looked at them with her frightened eyes, but Corrie was wild and remained in the offing, snorting and stamping.

Callum lost no time. The hind was light, and

he soon had her legs tied, then he hauled her on to the sled and roped her there. As the party moved off the young stag with the split ear stood as though frozen on the skyline, but night was falling fast and he was soon lost in the purple shadows.

They made a bed for Starpoint in a stall in the barn, with the two milk cows near for warmth and company. The children thawed the ice from her shoulders with warm oil, and Callum made a plaster which they fastened over the burnt area with sacking. It would be merely a matter of days for the wound to dry and clean, for young deer of Starpoint's age possess astounding powers of recovery.

Next morning they found Corrie back in the bracken field, so they spread hay for him. He was glad enough to accept the hay, but his trust in man was gone. He belonged now to one world, and to one world only—the rather tragic world of his own people. Yet he remained there till Starpoint was released from her hospital, a fit young beast again. Knowing the violence of red deer they had simply left the door open so that she was free to go when she chose. She took a long time about it: first came frightened eyes and long waving ears. She was "feared for the wolf on the other side," said Callum. Then came her long neck and the scarred shoulders, and finally she went out with a bound. Another bound and she was over the gate and with Corrie in the bracken field.

The two deer left immediately. They passed over the high boundary wall and remained in the bracken till darkness. There was no doubt where they were going. They descended to the road, then slipped into the Dead Forest by the big gap in the deer fence. They made their home about the tinkers' camping site, and it was surprising how little the great wood had changed. Had there been less wind at the time of the fire the whole of it would probably have gone up in smoke, but the roaring gale had simply cut channels through it, and the strength of the wind had prevented the fires running back or burning into the ground. There were huge patches of burnt heather in the Dead Forest; but in the Singing Forest only the tinder-dry branches were burnt, and the green roof overhead was left untouched. So the destruction was small, and the burned-out channels let the air among the tree-trunks, which in that way profited.

There were still dark corners where the deer could hide, and the needles underfoot were soft and silent to the tread. There was still the dense, weatherproof canopy overhead, so that even when the snow was blowing only a light dusting of it fell through to where they lay. They could hear the storms high above, but how different from the storms on the hill! They sang the softest of melodies through the green roof, the great pillars of the forest swinging almost imperceptibly as the soft surges of sound came and went. This place was really Corrie's home, and was to remain so all his days.

Soon they came to know the permanent residents of the wood, though some of them at first resented their presence. When they lay down by the tinkers' fireplace the red squirrels showered fir cones on them, but the two deer took no notice of the light bombardment, and after a time the squirrels went down to collect the cones they had dropped. Still the deer took no notice, and very soon the squirrels were scrambling over their bodies as they came and went. They learned that the coarse hair was warm to the feet, and it was pleasant to snuggle down under the big bodies or to sit on their heads to strip fir cones, while the scales showered down into the deers' eyes. If one of the deer shook its head at such times the squirrels would burst into a chattering and twittering tirade, but soon they were back again.

Wild creatures of different kinds cannot converse with one another, but it would seem that they have some means of thought-exchange supplemented by what they say. If so, there was not much to be learned from the conversations of the squirrels, for their thoughts were all mixed up, and they had no sooner started off on one theme than they were lost in another. They would be chattering about the jays which had stolen their favorite nest and were using it as their winter bedroom, when suddenly they would switch on to the water-snails in the brook, which were as sweet as nuts. Then magically the snails would turn into red-topped mushrooms, till snails and jays and nests and nuts became all mixed up in an incoherent jumble of chatter not even they themselves were understanding.

But the deer saw the squirrels only during the noon hours. As soon as the light went from the tree-tops they would dissolve into the gloom, and if the day were dark and wet they would not appear at all. The grey crows, on the other hand, belonged to the dusk and the darkness, and high up in their roosting-place they seemed unaware of Corrie and Starpoint who frequently rested under their great trees. But there was always a meaning in what *they* said, and something helpful to each other. One night the prevailing spokesman told of a dead whale washed up on the seashore some forty miles away, and the news provoked much cawing and excited wing-flapping. They told of dead deer lying in the remote washouts, and of a loch where the red-flanked trout were evidently smitten by disease, for their dead and dying lay in ridges along the silver sand of the margins. They told of high places and bitter shrieking winds where even the ptarmigan were burying themselves in the drifts, and such tales made the secure shelter of the wood even more gratifying. But perhaps it was the jays who brought the most welcome news; for they rasped and screeched at each other about the old barn where the old man across the river was feeding his ponies from a long manger, into which he poured the most delicious foods every morning at sunrise.

Thus, from a chance hint here and there, the wild creatures learn much from each other, and of all foods on earth Corrie loved oats the best.

It is impossible to say for certain how he came to know that they were available at that time, but he would not have left that beloved haunt had there been nothing better in the offing.

So it came about that one moonlight night he set off with determined step, and Starpoint had either to follow or be left behind. There was no wind, and they left the cathedral quietude of the great wood by the way they had entered it. At daybreak they lay down under an old stone wall where sheep were sheltering, and just across the field was the stable in which Ewen MacEwen kept his Shetland ponies. They slept in the stable these chill months, and the door of it was kept open.

Unfortunately for the red deer they can never remain long in one place, and it might be thought that they spend most of their lives looking for trouble. No two men think of them in the same light, for no two men see them in the same light. They are strange and whimsical gypsies, ruled by a thousand influences we cannot understand. No sooner do they find a place of shelter and plenty than they must leave it for some storm-swept land of hunger. No sooner are they safely in the woods than they must face the perils of the open slopes, where they know man's hand is raised against them; no sooner do they learn of danger in one place than they must go off and face exactly the same danger in another.

After years among them one learns much about their great wisdom, then suddenly the sidelights shift and the searchlights play at another angle, whereupon they sink to a pitiable level of incomprehension which places them lower than the mountain hares, incomparably lower than the little woodland roe. Perhaps it is for these very reasons, their unfathomableness, that of all wild creatures one comes to love the deer the best, for always there is a deep mystery behind their lives, and the longer one knows them the more does one realize how small the knowledge is and how small it must remain.

To Ewen MacEwen in his old age had fallen many light duties, among them the care of the Shetland ponies. He regarded them proudly as his own special charges, and this field towards the end of the Green Braes was a good place for them, because the deer habitually shunned these lower fields. Scores of deer fed in the field above the barn, but below it never, and rarely in the field where the barn stood.

The sun was shining brightly when next morning Ewen came along in his old Victorian ponytrap and, driving up to the barn, took the two long sacks of mixed oats and chaff from the back of it. At the sound of his arrival the Shetlands ran whinnying from the stable, and jostled round the heavy oak manger while he evenly emptied the sacks. After superficially tidying up and seeing to the drinking water he drove away, but looking back as he closed the gate he saw the two young deer eagerly feeding with the ponies, the young hind with the scarred shoulder-blades and the knobber with the red collar and the split ear. He did not in the least mind these two small creatures sharing the food, his only fear was that other deer might become bold enough to join them.

Nor was there long to wait for this; for next morning Ewen saw the horns of a big stag protruding above the ridge half a mile away and obviously watching him; so having performed his usual duties and driven off, Ewen made a point of returning and peering over the wall. Sure enough, the stag was at the manger feeding eagerly.

This might have been all right had the stag been a greyface, but he was not. He was one of those lop-eared, narrow-headed varmints with the crowded points, and Ewen rumbled disapprovingly. This went on for two or three days; then the old man began to notice horn abrasions on some of the ponies, so again he watched from a distance and saw the narrow-horned stag come down and promptly chase all the ponies from the manger, slashing at them with his horns. He was even too greedy to tolerate Corrie and Starpoint sharing with him, but since there were two sides to the trough they were nimble enough to keep him guessing.

Next morning Ewen fed the ponies at the manger inside the stable, and going back he was amused to watch Corrie coaxing the young hind to enter with him. She was fearful of another roof over her head, but at length she mastered her fears and the two of them went inside to feed with the ponies. Five minutes later the stag came down, but was afraid to enter the barn and finally went away.

Yet another morning, and to Ewen's surprise all the ponies were outside, hanging about the doorway as though afraid to enter. The old stalker went quietly up and peered in at the door to find the yellowface lying down in the straw, in majestic possession of the place. Instantly he scrambled up and presented his antlers, whereupon Ewen slammed and bolted the door. He now had the impudent stag safely impounded in the barn.

Forthwith Ewen went home and found the lariat he used for lowering shot stags down the steep mountain slopes. He also took a blackthorn stick of exceptional knobbiness, and thus armed he returned to the stable.

Ewen entered by a back way and mounted to the hayloft, while the stag snorted and stamped below. Skilled with a rope, it did not take the old man long to get a noose over the stag's antlers; then he hitched the rope over a rafter and progressively tightened it till the beast was half suspended by his horns, and he could do little more than dance about on his hind-legs. Ewen then went down with his blackthorn stick and gave the usurper a hammering he was not likely to forget.

When the rope was slacked and the door was opened, the stag made for the open hill faster than the old keeper had ever seen a stag run before. He took the march wall at a bound, then raced across the swamp heading for the heights of Corrie Rou, and it looked as though he would not stop till he got there. At all events he never again came down to feed with the ponies, and the story of how

Ewen pounded and hammered the big stag is told to this day in the valley.

Thus winter found Corrie and Starpoint as fit and well fed as any deer in the land, but it was noticeable that as the new hair grew on Starpoint's shoulders it was as white as mountain snow, a distinction that was to remain with her for all time. She became known as the saddle-backed hind, recognizable from afar, and generally in the company of the stag with the split ear.

As we have seen, the stags and the hinds of the glen country live entirely different lives, so much so that at times one would think they belong to different species. The hinds keep to the green corries and the sheltered terraces, for they have their calves to consider, and they hold together in their own little communities. The stags are completely independent, and generally consider no one but themselves. Wild, independent, and violent by nature, they seek the high and lonely hinterlands, often living apart from the hinds save for their period of activity in the autumn. Normally the hinds outlive them, for hinds are subject to none of the variations of the stags, the growing of new horns, the strenuous and often foodless periods of the rut when the King stags are too tormented by their rivals to feed and to take their rest. Winter finds them in poor condition to face its rigors, and many stags die on the hill long before they have reached their prime. All this particularly applies in the Corrie Rou country, that being hind country, while most of the stags winter in the hinterlands—just as Braemar is stag country, while for ten months of the year the hinds have the Spey valley slopes of the Cairngorms to themselves.

Such is the characteristic independence of red deer that they do not choose to rely upon man longer than they need. If there is natural food on the hill they will go to it rather than hang about man's threshold, even though they have to cover a much wider area to obtain what they need. In summer it is abundant on all sides and they can remain static, as Greyface and Corrie had done on the high slopes, but in winter it is more a matter of only a mouthful here and there, and they have to keep moving with shorter periods of rest. So it is not merely shortage of food that wears them down; it is the bitter combination of hunger and constant travel, particularly when there are many deer on the ground.

Satiated by the liberal gifts of man, Corrie and Starpoint duly returned to the hill, and with all the other deer mingling and moving to keep pace with their needs, it was surprising how soon the two drifted in with old friends, the grey-faced hinds. The little herd was still intact—old Grandma, Starpoint's mother, the hind with her face scarred by the wildcat's claws, and all the rest, just as they had been in the days of Greyface the Great.

That night the big swamp was again creeping with deer, and a soft wind from the north seemed to make them restless. Here and there an old hind would raise her head to test the air currents; a stag would stand up on his hind legs with head vertical as though he were browsing low foliage. The air became colder, till by midnight it was bitterly cold. Herd after herd the deer began to drift out of the swamp on the upwind side. Some were heading for the upper valley, some for the big woods, some for the forbidden plantings, but Corrie and Starpoint knew where they were going, and struck out on their own.

The river was in full and loaded with moving ice, not pleasant for a deer to cross in this bitter wind, so Corrie started down the steep and stony pathway which eventually joined the occupation road near Ewen's lodge. The multitudinous clicking of hoofs behind him caused him to look round, and he saw that all the grey-faced hinds were sedately following him. And he saw, too, that the big ungainly yellow-faced stag which had forced its way into Ewen's pony stable was bringing up the tail end of the procession; for he was cunning enough to realize that the two calves knew something about the lie of the country. Where they led it might be worth his following, for they belonged here.

None of the herd wanted him, certainly not the hinds, for they knew enough about the arrogance and intolerance of old yellowface stags. As soon as they reached the occupation road, indeed, with the light of Ewen's cottage back across the orchard, old Grandma made their feelings clear by standing broadside across the road, with head indignantly upheld. So she faced up to their big follower, and clearly she said to him: "Now, are you going back? because we do not want you with *us!*"

Had he been a proud stag he would have done one of two things—either he would have beaten her for her impudence, or he would have respected her sex and withdrawn from the herd. The yellow-face who had returned to slay Starpoint would probably have beaten her; the great Greyface would have nibbled the grass at the roadside, and left her and her herd to their own devices. But this stag had no pride. He simply barged straight past her and joined the herd beyond, grunting over his shoulder that for two pins he would throw her into the river. Great in body he assuredly was, but his narrow brow and long and ungainly limbs bore evidence that he would never be great in being.

They came in due course to the white gate by the keeper's lodge with the main road beyond, and following Corrie the whole herd lightly crossed the low wall at the side of it, wriggling their bodies between the two strands of wire held by iron posts above the coping stones. They passed swiftly on with scarcely a sound, but the big stag in the rear behaved with the blundering awkwardness they might have expected. He should have gone over the top, instead of which he tried to pass between the wires as the rest had done. His horns caught in the top wire, and having failed to force a way through he fell back into the road. The din and clatter he made was tremendous, and wakened the dogs in the kennels. The herd went on, no doubt hoping he would remain on the wrong side of the wall.

With the faintest rattle of hoofs they crossed the bridge of many arches, and soon the castle gates were on their left, the lane to the sawmill opposite. Corrie, of course, knew every inch of the way, and ahead of them now stretched the main street of the village, with the four street lights it boasted still gleaming unnaturally.

Most of the hinds were distinctly nervous, and the little knot of deer tightened more closely at Corrie's heels. Even Starpoint pressed closer to him for reassurance, but Corrie with head held high was on his own ground, and not for a moment did his courage waver. The windows were darkened, and he knew the villagers had gone to ground for the night. A black cat flashed across the road, and sent a fresh shudder through the herd; then the sound of hoofs behind them signified that the yellowface had eventually got through, and with characteristic disregard for caution was speeding to join them. He did so with a clatter that caused the whole herd to break into a trot, and Grandma snorted eloquently.

Soon they had passed the last house and reached the Singing Forest; and Corrie chose to enter by the break in the deer fence which the roe-deer had shown them on the day of the fire. He and Star-point slipped quickly through, but the break was small for most of the hinds. Each of them enlarged it a little, while the whole fence swung and the high steel posts vibrated noisily. Presently they were all through and safely in the wood—all but the big stag, who would never have attempted the gap had he been a beast of average intelligence.

As might have been expected, his efforts were deplorable. He tried to force his way through, but his horns caught up and there he stuck, struggling desperately to free himself. The whole fence teetered for forty feet on either side, and from the depth of the wood came the terrier-like warning of a roe. The stag regained his legs and shook him-self, but it was of no use. He was firmly held by the horns and his struggles merely drew the knotted wires tighter.

The rest of the herd went on—to the gypsy camping place—and scarcely had they shaken the light snow from their coats when the expected storm broke. It came suddenly through the tree-tops, scattering a shower of pine needles on the backs of the deer. The big trees shook to their very roots, and the bitter cold of it could be felt

even there in the stillness. But over the general
tumult they could still hear the ping of taut wires
as the stag on the roadway sought to free himself.
Poor brute! He would perish within an hour out
there.

Corrie was anxious, and after a time he could
stand it no longer. The hinds had settled for the
night, but the young stag was still conscious that
one of the herd was missing. The grey-faced stags
are always anxious for the welfare of their herd
males, which is a sign of true leadership, so after
a time Corrie went back to look for him, and Starpoint went with him.

They found the big stag as they had left him,
still held by the horns, but he was red-eyed and
unapproachable, though the two youngsters did
not sense the danger. Corrie went up to sniff him,
thinking to encourage him, but received a blow
that gashed his face from eye to nostrils. It dashed
him back against the screen, and almost simul-
taneously the yellowface struck at Starpoint.

It was a terrible blow, for he caught her in the
full swing of his antlers, and the click and thud of
it was wicked to hear. She, too, was thrown against
the wire, through which the stag made a further
desperate effort to force his way.

Then Corrie saw red. Such rage as he had never felt before throbbed every fiber of his small being, and he drew back against the screen to fight. His horns were mere spikes, but they were hard and sharp as needles. He had never used them before, and not till that moment was he really aware of their presence. Instinct told him where to strike, and he struck with all his force. He launched his whole strength into it, leaping high to catch the yellowface behind the foreleg. And the blow went home with all his weight and strength behind it.

The blow went home and the hot blood gushed over Corrie's face and into his eyes, but his own weight was not sufficient to withdraw the dagger points. He braced his fore-hoofs against the flank of his enemy, and the yellowface gave a gigantic upward bound which tore the wire like calico, and for one moment he hung poised, his fore-hoofs over the top of the fence, seven feet up, while Corrie staggered into the thickets. Then the big stag fell back, but again his horns caught up, this time in the topmost strands, and he hung there.

The grey hinds knew what had happened. They knew from the blood on Corrie's face, and by the way the two young deer trembled. They mothered them into the warmth of the fold, mothered them against their bodies, while during a break in the storm the skies became aflame with the wildfire of the Aurora. To Corrie it was pleasant to be mothered in this way, for while Starpoint could go to her own mother, he had no memories of motherhood.

Next day the herd broke up, because the scent of death was about this place and they were afraid to stay. Here again was the wolf-fear, for wolves feed upon the dead, and it was not wise for the living to remain there.

It was the forester who, next day, found the big stag, rigid but still swinging. He was puzzled by the two puncture marks under the forelegs, more puzzled still when he found Corrie's red collar lying on the ground below. The string binding was rotten and had broken, as it was intended to break. The collar was weatherworn and ragged, and later in the day he handed it over to Callum. Now it hangs in the nursery with its story attached—or rather some of the story, confined mainly to a mere statement of facts.

❦ ❦ ❦

CHAPTER 9

No wild animals are born great, none has great-ness thrust upon it. A leader becomes a leader sim-ply because he has won the confidence of those about him. He is elected by common ballot, by the world-old law of selection and elimination. But greatness is a thing of the soul. One may come to know many clever wild beasts which are far from being great. In all probability they are cunning and sly, treacherous and untrustworthy, whereas the great are open in disposition, ready with their caresses, eager to take the burden of peril upon themselves. The soft-mouthed old fool Bongo was great among dogs, and Greyface was great among stags, but as a rule it is hard to recognize the individual over the span of life whereby we might assess its worth. Corrie we were to know about the home woods by his split ear, and I believe he became great among the red deer, for he possessed outstandingly the blessed gift of faithfulness. In this respect he was greater than Greyface.

Early that spring Corrie "cast," or rather the two swelling lumps of his new horns pushed out his juvenile prongs, and during this process he became restless and fretful, apt to strike at Starpoint without provocation, and uncertain where to go. For a few days he could not rest anywhere or decide anything, so Starpoint took command. The first primroses found them making their quarters about the old burnt-out clachan.

It was one of the most shut away and secluded corners of the forest, yet almost daily they saw a small human figure there. She wore a tartan shawl and carried a small blue basket over her arm—the kind the gypsy craftsmen used to make in their better days. She was, in fact, a gypsy child, and her brightly colored clothing indicated that indeed she *did* belong to the basket-making clans. Always she was passing along the old road from the clachan to the village, a way which had sunk into disuse ever since the clachan was abandoned. It is said that one of the old women secretly destroyed it after an epidemic of smallpox. She set fire to the heather roofs when the rest of her people were away, but she forgot that one child still lay sick in one of the hovels. So the story goes, but it is all so strange that only the known facts can be recorded.

On this old road, near to the clachan, stood the Pine Ridge, a favorite haunt of the giant grouse, known in Gaelic as capercailzie, "horse of the woods." Of late these great birds had become too plentiful, and were playing havoc in the young plantings. Accordingly, Alastaire frequently went that way with his .22 rifle, generally in the early mornings when the cocks were apt to sit in the branches lost in the ecstasy of their saw-saw love song. At such times they could be stalked if one watched their movements carefully.

That Easter morning Alastaire was cautiously mounting the hill when, nearing the ridge of pines, he saw the two young deer lying down under the trees, and he knew that if he bounded them all chance of sport would be gone. Therefore he dropped down into the bracken, thinking that, as they scented him, they would move quietly away.

He had been there only a few moments when the small girl appeared over the rise, her tartan shawl over her head, her blue basket over her arm. He recognized the tartan as that of the Mackenzie basket-makers, and the boy slipped his hand into his sporran in search of the chocolate he usually carried, thinking to share it with her when she passed.

But when he looked up again there was no child there. This did not surprise him greatly, for he knew the shyness of the gypsies. Undoubtedly she had seen him and quickly turned back on realizing that they would come face to face. Then he saw that the two deer were still there, still placidly chewing the cud, though he quite clearly recalled that they had started and turned their heads in her direction as she passed only a few yards away. Probably they were quite accustomed to her passing on her daily messages to the village.

Later in the day Alastaire spoke about it to Callum, asking if the Mackenzie "tinklers" were camping in the big wood, at which Callum regarded him thoughtfully and shook his head. He replied in the Gaelic that the basket-makers no longer visited this glen, and awaited further information.

"I am sure it was one of them I saw on the Pine Ridge this morning," Alastaire told him. "A girl about Fiona's age, but her shawl was Mackenzie."

"And what like was this wee girl?" Callum asked eagerly, and Alastaire described her minutely.

Callum spread his big hands. "So you have seen her, Master Alastaire!" he said quietly. "But she is not a child—not as Miss Fiona and the other girls we know are children, because she grows no older. The children of the valley grow up and marry, and many of them move to distant places, but she does not grow up, and year after year she is still there. My grandfather saw her, my father saw her, and I saw her when I was a boy. Now you have seen her in your boyhood, just as she has been since the old clachan was destroyed. My grandfather knew her as a living child, and he was among the old people who said that she was Morag Mackenzie, the child who perished in the fire. Always we have known her as Morag."

Being a Highland boy Alastaire was not unduly

surprised at this. He merely thought a few moments, then he said—"That accounts for one queer thing, Callum—the deer were not afraid of her, though they watched her pass quite close to them. They did not move."

"They would not be afraid," said Callum. "The deer see many things and understand many things we cannot see or understand. They stand and look at nothing, then either they move towards it or they turn away, according to whether it is good or evil. They are fey, unfathomable, superstitious. I have watched a whole herd following something we could not see, and blind to all else about them."

The boy nodded. "I know," he admitted, "they are strange and whimsical beasties, but father always says that their suspicions are mainly due to their inherited wolf-fear."

"That is true, Master Alastaire," Callum was quick to admit. "But it is not the wolf-fear that prevents their feeding on the Green Braes below the old barn. There is some of the sweetest grazing in that part of the valley, but the deer have shunned the place as far back as living memory goes. Hunger will not drive them to it, though history tells us that it was once their favorite feeding ground. Then the feud broke out between the laird and his tenants over the killing of deer, and the clans rose in all their strength to form a mighty army. They came from the glens and the valleys and the mountain meadows, and they drove the deer in one vast herd to cross the river at their crossing by the great white stone. There they massacred them by the hundred till the river ran red. Even now the plough turns up their bones, and that is not the only scene of tragedy, Master Alastaire, to which the deer have never returned."

Corrie, meanwhile, had outgrown much of his hind-like rotundity, and was assuming the more rugged but graceful lines of the stag. He became higher in the withers and more compact in the hindquarters, and when his new horns grew each was complete with a brow point, so that he became a perfect little stag. From his general build and the width of his horns Ewen prophesied that he would make a Royal.

He was changing in character, too, less disposed to run at the bark of a sheep dog, or to turn tail at the approach of a King stag. He ceased to watch for himself, but left the ever-faithful Starpoint to do the watching. She would lie on a high point above and keep close count of all their surroundings, just as a year ago he had watched for

Greyface, except that she was infinitely more scrupulous and thorough. Again it was Starpoint who decided the routine of the day, while Corrie fell in lazily behind her, and not always could she induce him to hurry when there was real danger behind them. She would stand above, stamping and snorting as she looked back at him, but he would just step indifferently along as though they had a whole week to think about it. He had to know the whole facts of the case before he was prepared to hurry, and it took even more to make him panic.

When the flies became bad it was Starpoint who set the pace for the upward climb, and the ascent was not so leisurely an affair as he and Greyface had made of it. They went by the heights of Corrie Rou into a land of terrible grandeur, where there were black little lochs hidden among the precipices, some of them desolately beautiful. This country must have been timbered at one time, part of the old Caledonian forests which extended high into the hills, for the roots of gigantic trees littered the loch margins, looking like mighty octopuses spreading their black tentacles to the sun. Giant trout were believed to haunt some of these volcanic pools, but they were too inaccessible for boats to be carried to them, and their shores too steep for safety. There was also a bubbling caldron of ruddle, the red ochre which the shepherds used for marking their sheep. Although it was reputed to be of much finer quality than any of the factory-produced ruddles it was too difficult of access to be worth the bother.

Constantly that summer the two young deer fed among the drifting clouds, for they climbed higher and higher as the grass grew. One would have thought that not even a mountain goat could have reached the giddy shelves to which they climbed. But up there they frequently saw the small red deer that shelter in the caves and feed in winter on the landslides which bring the Alpine plants rolling down from still more inaccessible places. These kept to themselves, frequently grazing on shelves which even Corrie and Starpoint could not gain. Their horns were small and as red as their bodies, little thicker than a man's thumb where they left the coronet, and they could leap and scramble from shelf to shelf when there appeared to be insufficient steerage for a marten. When the eagle appeared they would vanish from the cliff-faces as does the vanishing mist.

At night time the mountain foxes yelled and

moaned on all sides of them, and the "yoch-yoch" of the grey crows and the "yoich-yoich" of the ravens never ceased from twilight to twilight. Once, far below, they watched a wildcat picking her way across a burn, and even at that distance she looked the size of a leopard.

They drifted westward towards the wide terraces and the tablelands, and though neither of them had been that way before they knew exactly where they were. Perhaps they went in search of the grey hinds, for duly they found them, and Star-point ran straight to her mother, who had a new calf running at her heels. But Corrie gave the herd no more than a passing glance, then he strode majestically on, and without even a backward look for his faithful partner. One might have thought that he had come there purely to shed her; and as though there was a tacit understanding between them, she did not attempt to follow. So Corrie went on alone into the storms and shadows of stag country.

Corrie was lost to sight for some weeks, at the time of the year when the prettiest scenes occur in hind country. Only a small number of the hinds brought their calves into the world at those high altitudes; the great majority were born on the heathered slopes where those graceful ladies of the woods, the silver birch trees, grew. There, at sunrise and sunset, one might have seen scores and scores of the dappled calves playing, their mothers watching from the nearby ridges, but for the most part unseen. Here and there the little blue tercel hawk uttered his calls to his mate, a titlark in his claws, or a mountain blackbird sang his wild and gusty song from his rowan tree above the burn.

Over in stag country it was different. It was a land of great distances and stony heights, with the ladders of heaven streaming between the storms to light up the soul-searching loneliness of small deep valleys, so far away that man seldom explored them. Here and there were herds of stags lost in the vastnesses, but soon the time came when herd joined herd along the stony pathways, all of them drifting northwards, as though they had agreed to meet. But if that were so they had agreed only to disagree.

October came again with its mad surge of new life, with the clicking of cloven hoofs and the melee of horns and heads. Their horns were clean, and many of them were already humped and black from their soiling-pools. Corrie was early over with the rush, and he seemed to know exactly where to go. Instinct must have led him, for he had come to know hind country well in his calf-hood. He slipped away from the general turmoil of Corrie Rou, and slunk unnoticed into the hidden little valley of the hazels. There he found the herd of the grey-faced hinds, supplemented by many of the hind calves with whom he had played last year. They seemed almost to be awaiting his arrival.

If so, it must have been difficult to realize that this was the Corrie of Corrie Rou who had worn the red collar; for he burst into their midst like a bellowing gladiator, making the rocky sides of the narrow caldron ring with his thunder. Hidden away there they had missed the combing of the promiscuous army from over the heights, and Corrie had no rivals. His roars were continuous as he approached, and he dragged his fore-hoofs to increase the clatter. The hot breath gushed from his gaping maw, and his horns were thrust back on his withers. He might have been some terrible foe come to annihilate the whole herd, yet the hinds merely looked at him admiringly, then turned their heads coyly aside.

Soon he was absorbed into the embrace of the

herd, and his vitality was astounding. He mated with Starpoint many times, till she would no longer stand for him and the other hinds gathered round, thrusting each other jealously aside as they awaited their turns. Carelessly, apparently unwittingly, they placed themselves at his disposal, and impartially he passed from hind to hind, the general excitement seeming to stimulate those who at first had no interest in him. So it went on for some days, and for a young beast Corrie did his work heroically for the declining race of greyface deer. Truly he had benefited by the good living of his calfhood days, and since it is the young beasts who throw the best stag calves, it is not to be wondered at that herds deteriorate when artificial feeding becomes impossible.

Then the herd passed out of the valley of the hazels and scattered into the wildernesses of the great caldron, and Corrie joined up with a herd of young beasts which had found their way into the high plantings. The Indian summer lingered long into the autumn, and while the many-colored mushrooms still dotted the mossy banks, Corrie joined up with the grey-faced ten-pointer who, had he known it, was the second-in-command that night when the big yellowface turned back to slay Starpoint.

There was little indication of their friendship except that they grazed side by side. Together they sought the great piles of rotting sawdust that lay under the wooden walls of an old sawmill. The dust was still balsam scented, and it was pleasant to lie in it, insulated from the cold earth, tossing it over their shoulders with their fore-hoofs till it trickled through their coarse hair and they could feel it coolly on their skins. Other stags, old and young, joined them as they left the rut, most of them young beasts, for the old stags seemed more readily inclined to wander back into stag country.

Corrie had good faith in his well-knit and alert companion, and it is more than likely that they were blood relations. On all sides were yellow-faced stags, long limbed and angular, donkey-eared and moose-snouted, but they were clearly a different clan, though all mixed contentedly together.

But pleasant though the days of the Indian summer were, the young stags knew that its caress was only transient. In body they were idle but at heart they were restless, and they merely waited for a leader to take them on a great journey. All were spent stags, and winter was close upon them.

Their coats lacked luster; they were still humped in the back and they felt the cold. The faintest breeze and they would gather round the sawmill for shelter. Their eyes lacked sheen, and when they lay down their eyelids drooped wearily. Then came a soft breeze from the sea, and instantly a change came over the herd. All of them rose; some stood high on their hind-hoofs and sniffed the breeze as the old hinds had done that night when the yellowface was hung in the deer fence.

The ten-pointer moved to the fore, Corrie behind him, and behind Corrie followed more than twenty stags.

It was not a deer highway by which they went, but a number of single and deeply trodden tracks, exactly parallel and running across the mountain face. Below them stretched the great haugh—the waste swamplands which filled the valley to the sea, and the fact that their way consisted of a number of paths, rather than a single highway, indicated that when the deer passed that way they did so in numbers, not as a single herd. For deer traveling in numbers must fan out in order to feed on the way, since if they moved in single file the vanguard would pluck up every morsel of food, and those behind would find the roadside bare.

They went down the valley by the hill route high above the river, and that night in the moonlight they passed on through a lovely region of old heather, clothed with Scots firs as far as the eye could reach. They snatched their food on the way, progressing easily, and at daybreak they still moved on, the journey being without incident. Once a peregrine swooped at a grouse which fell on the path in front of the leader, who picked it up and marched on munching steadily, the wings of the bird hanging down on either side of his jaws. Once the screaming of a rabbit in a snare took half a dozen stags striding eagerly to that place. Between them they tore the rabbit to pieces, each chewing his share contentedly—for the corner fangs of the red deer are evidence of a once carnivorous diet.

At length the herd passed down with the descending moors into a wide desert of marran grass, juniper and buckthorn, and here a very distinct pathway led into the blue distance, furrowed with wheel tracks. It was no more than a sandy desert track, but giant buckthorn overgrew it on either side. For a thousand ages it had been a deer path to the sea, for here a dozen deer roads, such as the one our herd had followed, united to cross the barren stretch. Of late, man had adopted it as a road for the holiday-makers down to the sands: to the deer it was still their own road.

Darkness was closing in as they took the sandy track, and above them the blue skies extended into a distance which foretold blue sea beyond. The ten-pointer leading was cautious and ill at ease. He seemed to suspect the lurking of a wolf behind every buckthorn. Constantly he shied aside and collided with those pressing nervously about him. This was strange country. He may have been that way before, but he knew it to be dangerous country. Nor were his instincts far wrong, for presently they sniffed the approach of other deer, and the two herds united.

The news of the new herd was not good news. They must have left the hills later than our herd, but they had come by the bottom lands route which Corrie and Greyface had taken, and somewhere they had met with disaster. The smell of blood was upon their coats, and one of them was dragging a shattered hind-hoof. They were all stags, a frightened and disorganized little party, glad to fall in at the heels of the ten-pointer.

Among them was the infant—the stag calf Corrie knew, the little fellow Callum had dragged through the deer fence—still sticking to the men of his own kind, though he should have been with his mother among the hind herds. He made no pretense at being a grown stag, but was glad to remain the infant of the party. He ran over to Corrie in instant recognition and raised his face. Corrie licked him and tucked him under his side, bidding him stay there and make himself small. This was dangerous country—which surely the infant already knew.

The sandy track snaked in and out, winding round stagnant pools still brackish from the spring tides and foul with rotting vegetation in the hollows. The sea wind cast eddies of sand into their nostrils, hindering their sense of smell. They could smell only the enticing and alluring sea. They pressed on easily, over thirty deer now, but with the wind in their nostrils, pressing eagerly seaward and, deer-like, they forgot their back trail.

The powerful car came silently round the bend behind them. The occupants of it had marked them down and knew they would stick to the deer road. They were lawless men, whose forefathers for ages past had taken toll of horn, feather and liquor. This was to be their second raid that night on beasts down from the hills.

As the car rounded the corner its headlights

and spotlights blazed out, illuminating the closely packed herd ahead. Then came the *tock-tock* of an army rifle, followed by the *brrr* of an automatic. The bullets cast up vast spumes of sand and burred away into the distance, but there was the dead thud of bullets which struck, and deer were going down on all sides.

They were bewildered by the glare, by the din, by the spumes of rising sand. Some stood still and looked back into the eyes of death. Others broke on either side, and a few turned towards the car. It was merely a matter of firing into the brown of the herd, and it was just what these men with their blackened faces and bloody hands were looking for.

Round the deer was the white glare of the bushes, bewildering them so that they did not know which way to run. The scent of blood grew stronger, and they broke in all directions, colliding with each other, trampling over their wounded. At Corrie's feet lay the ten-pointer, coughing out his life. The calf ran hither and thither, uttering his shrill cries and buffeted from one to another. Some rose and fell and rose again, their broken legs crumpling under them. Corrie gained the shadows, miraculously unscathed, and looked back into the glare. He saw the bloody carnage of it, and screamed through his nostrils for the survivors to come to him. They came, a miserable few, and thundered behind him through the dark alleyways of the undergrowth; and glued to his side was the infant.

The herd left the sandhills and took to the sea-shore, sheering off to avoid a gaily colored but deserted line of bathing-huts and caravans. Daylight had come, and in this land there was no cover. They might well have wondered why they had come to so terrible a region.

Corrie was leading, and the cliffs now rose above them. They were low cliffs, and about them the petrels still glided and hung. Corrie led the way close under the cliffs, still following the old deer path which had led them from the Corrie Rou.

They came to a great cave high above spring-tide level. A deer path led up from the mouth of it, zigzagging up the cliff face to the summit, deeply trodden and as old as any deer path in the kingdom. At the mouth of the cave an old yellow-face hind met them, and behind her in the gloom they could see her sisters. Far back in the darkness they could scent and hear running water; for deer must have water when they go down to the salt sea.

The hinds were most concerned with the infant, for his coat was sprayed with blood. To them the scent of blood was the scent of death, and they could not convince themselves that he was un-injured. They held a committee meeting over him and in turn sniffed him from end to end. They looked into each other's faces and butted each other and told each other not to interfere. Then one by one they licked him from end to end till his coat was sodden and he got sick of it. He laid back his ears and butted them and struck at them with his fore-hoofs, till he had driven every hind out of the cave and was free to join up with the stags, who were already far down on the beach, nosing out the daintiest morsels of weed for the iodine they needed.

There was that one particular moss-like weed growing in the crevices of the rocks for which they nosed ravenously. It was sweet yet sour, mellow yet acrid, and they went about with the roots of it trailing from their mouths. The fishermen of that coast call it hindweed.

At sundown thirst drove the stags back to the

cave for fresh water. They drank as strangers to the art, dipping their noses repeatedly at the crystal pool, then raising their heads as though they wondered at the taste of it. Back there in the cold shadows water dripped from the roof of the cave where mica crystals and phosphorescent sea-shells glistened.

The bellies of the deer were extended with sea fare, for they had munched crustaceans in addition to devouring weed. Only the infant was not interested in such food, because his body did not yet need it. Some day he would—and he would remember the roads that led to the sea.

Meantime he was nostalgic, and wanted only to be away. He had been in two bloody massacres in the past twelve hours, and he wanted to return to the familiar shelters of the Corrie Rou. That night he became frightened, because a great bearded beast came in from the unknown sea, and looked with water-washed eyes into the darkness of the cave. It blew the seawater from its nostrils and came waddling into the cave with a gait which in itself was terrifying. The infant fled back into the darkness crying, till they heard him fall into the pool. But the stags and hinds paid no heed to the great grey seal, and others, and yet others of his kind followed the old bull into the cave, to lie among the hinds, absorbing their warmth and regardless of their presence, as they had been through the ages.

But the stags rested little because they were licking the brine-soaked walls of the cave. They licked steadily all night, and had one looked at those walls one would have seen that the salt-impregnated stratas of lime were licked into pockets and hollows by the tongues of generations of deer. At intervals they went to the pool to drink.

They remained next day, but when night came the infant was persistent. He whipped Corrie and the herd of stags together by his constant appeals, and mounting the cliff path he looked back to see if they were following. To his surprise they were all following a miserable remnant of those that had left the Corrie Rou.

It was the infant who led them—not because he was best able to lead, but because he was determined to go. The stags fell in behind him because it was easier to follow than to lead, but the little fellow proved an able leader. He was bright-eyed and alert, and seemed to be conscious of his duties. They passed over the low cliffs into a region of stunted and frosted heather, scored by dry and barren little valleys. He led them high up the slopes, so that they could see all round but were never exposed above the skyline. Often the calf stopped and for long periods looked searchingly on all sides. Once Corrie nudged him on, at which he turned and struck at Corrie. He had good cause too, for presently they all saw the car without lights moving slowly across the sandhills.

So cautiously did the infant lead that the sun was up before they left the sandhills, and ahead stretched the desolate swamps of the long valley. Not a mile to the south lay the brackish loch which Corrie and Greyface had visited, so that Corrie could have taken over now and led them by an established deer path back to the Corrie Rou. But the infant had evidently come this way with his ill-fated herd, for he knew every step of it. Perhaps he knew more, for he did not spare them. He led them at a brisk trot all day, and by sundown they crossed the river by the great white stone. No old hind could have led them better, and in the wood that night Corrie and the infant slept side by side. But there an empty place at the other side of Corrie, the place which the ten-pointer had occupied.

❋ ❋ ❋

CHAPTER 10

The old planting was full of deer, mainly stags who should have moved on at the end of the rut. The Indian summer and the abundance of food had tempted them to stay on, for run stags would remain round a haystack in the middle of the Sahara without an anxious thought till they had eaten the last wisp of it. Then they would curse each other, give up hope, and finally die clannishly huddled together.

No doubt they meant to get out tomorrow, or the next day, but a roaring northeaster came in that no deer would have faced on the Height of Land. Scores of them huddled round the sawmill, while its sides clanked and its rusty doors swung on their hinges. At the root of every great tree the stags lay touching, placidly allowing themselves to be drifted over. When the storm abated winter had sealed the high ridges, and there was no road over the heights of the Corrie Rou. Throughout the glen country thousands of deer were trapped by snow in valleys to which they did not belong.

More winds blew and more snows fell. The village became isolated and the villagers fell to living on each other's flour bins and to taking in each other's washing. Over the country provisions were being dropped from the air, but there was no food for the starving deer, which were destroying the plantings wholesale. Ewen MacEwen, having wallowed through the snow to take the census of the woods, shook his head despondently, stating that the deer would die by the hundreds unless food could be found for them; but the laird pointed out that so would the sheep and cattle unless rain fell or hay descended from heaven. How could they feed such a starving multitude when even the hill sheep had hardly strength to drag themselves into the shelters?

Deer were buried shoulder-deep in the drifts, and the grey crows came down and took the eyes out of them while they were still living. The rivers and the burns became corridors of ice, sealing in the salmon till their white hulks drifted with the pan-ice in every backwash. The gullies were piled and pillared with ice, clinging to the sides till their edges almost met. Looking into those inky dungeons was like looking into a nightmare pit, where a single misstep would have plunged the unwary. At school and at home the children were warned that of all things they must not go near the river, for the water spirits were there in thousands and would assuredly get them. In the lower woods the leaf-mold rose into grave-like mounds, and through the crisp surface one sank to the knees. Small birds fled seawards, and only the crows and the ravens prospered, for when others are dying that is their harvest-time.

One night almost a hundred starving deer crashed through the old deer fence at the bottom of the plantings, and crossed the frozen river. There is no record about the stag who led them, but they wallowed through the drifts to the Singing Forest.

Reaching the deer fence their misfortunes began. The drifts were piled clean over it, and they could not find the gap. Here and there the top of the fence showed above the snow, but the drifts yielded under the deer and they sank helplessly. They trod out deep tunnels, but only to collide with the wire-screen under the snow. They tried to force a way through it, crowding each other, but the drifts descended upon them and buried them. Many of them were already so weak that they were trampled, and did not emerge. Their hoofs were worn to the quick by pawing at the icy ground.

A few of the old hinds stood back, watching the pathetic drama. It was clear there was no way through, and they turned reluctantly away. The rest fell in behind them, not knowing where they were going, following blindly and dead to all sense of fear.

They made for the Strath road, where the deepest drifts were clear, and gathered there, undecided which way to turn. Then Corrie set off to the right, behind him Starpoint, the rest of the forlorn party at her heels. They were heading for the village, trampling out a deep channel down the middle of the road, till they gained the first houses and the going was easier.

They passed the old grey schoolhouse, and the children were let out of the classroom to see them pass. The deer stared wide-eyed at the human beings, but trod steadily on. Rank after rank they went by, knowing that in their enfeebled state man would not raise his hand against them. Callum's little son knew some of them from what his father had told him, and was able to point them out to his schoolmates. Corrie and Starpoint they knew, and when the infant trotted by a cheer went up for him, for he was the youngest, yet among the ablest. Their hearts went out to them, and to the broken stag who fell at the school gates and did not try to rise. The children crowded round him, and shared their little luncheon packets with him, bannock and apples and gingerbread, which he accepted gratefully; and when all the others were passed he scrambled to his legs and, sliding a good deal, went after them.

When the herd reached the village crossroad they resembled a pathetic deputation of survivors gathered there to exhort man's aid. The villagers stood at their doorways, but they had nothing to give, and could only watch sad-eyed while the procession trod sadly on. The minister called his people about him, and they stood bareheaded while the old man offered up a prayer for the starving deer. It was a poignant little ceremony, and many an eye was moist as they sang their closing hymn. All of them were glad that the minister had thought to do this, for only the Almighty could now save these tottering beasts from the terrors of winter.

The herd passed through the village, turned at the high-boundary wall and crossed the bridge of many arches. Then they struck off upstream to their recognized crossing at the timbered island. An old grey hind was leading now, and several of the villagers were following to help those that failed in the drifts. Some they dragged into their hen houses and outbuildings in the hope of saving them with what little they had.

The old hind stood and looked across the frozen channel to the island, and at the steep wall of ice on the other side. She could only judge by what she herself could do, and she saw that the crossing was beyond her, therefore it was beyond the power of her followers. Reluctantly she went on to search for an easier crossing higher up the river, and with her went the other grey hinds, and Corrie, Starpoint and the infant.

The other deer had crowded up to the crossing, and among them was a gaunt stag with narrow horns whose length of leg favored him. It was he who broke herd law, for he knew that he could cross, but that those who followed must take their chance. He strode in where their leader had refused to lead, and the frantic creatures behind him followed.

The stag crossed easily and scrambled up the icy wall on the other side, crashing through the rim of ice and leaving it no easier for those behind him. He gained the high bank above, and looked back, and soon he was to see what he had done.

His immediate followers tried to rush the crossing, and some of them fell as the ice went through under their combined weight. The green water welled up through the rift, and some were overwhelmed. The rest fought on till they reached the icy wall on the other side, then disaster struck fast and furiously.

The leaders had no space for movement, and as they scrambled to mount, more and more of the shelf crumbled under them. They came crashing down on to the heads of those below, who in turn could not retreat because of the jostling mob scrambling from the water. They were trampling each other hideously, forcing each other back into the cold stream, while still the desperate mob came up to add to the confusion. There were piles and ridges of deer trampling and struggling under the ice-lip and out into the deep water.

The men standing by could do no more than

mutter, "Poor brutes! Poor brutes!" It seemed that the whole herd was doomed to annihilation— all but the grey hinds and those following them, who stood under the trees watching. The big stag on the other side was also watching.

There was a shout from the hillside behind, and they saw Callum with his rifle—Callum who was responsible for the deer and knew more about them than any other man in the glen. He waved the men to move aside, for they were trying to turn the herd; then Callum threw up his rifle, and they saw the spit and recoil of it, steady against his shoulder. Also they saw the stag on the other side of the river crumple up, then slide head foremost into the turmoil of his own making.

Following the scream of the bullet there came a lull which was almost breath-taking, for clearly it signified a crisis. Callum had shot down the leader who, standing above, had served as a beacon for the rest to follow. Now his tortured herd males had seen him fall, had seen him slide down into destruction, so that they were left without a leader. And during that dramatic pause they ceased to be a blind mob, and the wisest of them turned back across the river.

The rest rallied and followed. They surged back through the broken ice, in which many were still struggling and sinking hopelessly, but the main tragedy was over. They broke into the drifts and sank, and the rescue squads of young men got to work. Then the little knot of grey hinds under the trees turned upstream, leaving the scene of the tragedy.

Callum remained at the crossing, superintending the loading of exhausted deer into a transport lorry, to be taken to the bracken field. A party of young people came down from the castle, wearing their well-cut tweeds, and some of them with skis slung over their shoulders. They wanted to help, but Callum told them that little could be done unless someone could miraculously produce a load or two of turnips and a few bales of hay. One of them mentioned that the minister's prayers, appropriate though they had been, had hardly met with an immediate response, to which Callum replied that the Almighty does not work in such ways. One could not expect an old man's prayer to go rocketing straight up to the throne of heaven, to be answered like a prepaid telegram, but ere long they would see whether or not the prayer was heard. For Callum that day had seen the mountain hares drifting uphill.

A mile up the river the grey hinds crossed on a gravel bed, the hollow ice crunching crisply under their hoofs. They passed into the dreary whiteness of the upper slopes, but if there was any green under the snow and ice it was nibbled naked by the rabbits. The stars shone brightly as they wandered on, seeking the wind-swept channels, till it seemed as though the leading hind was following a scent-line. Every few paces her nose went down, and the pace was quickening. She was following the scent of a roe-deer, for the roe knew their way about the low country better than deer from the hill.

They came to an old barn on a wind-swept ridge. The snow had drifted over the roof of it, and it looked as though a row of little peak-capped gnomes were peering over the roof ridge, watching the approaching deer. On the storm side of the building the drift of snow extended to the eaves, but the roe had trampled a gangway through it, terminating in a black square half-way up the wall, the hole through which hay was forked.

Here Corrie took the lead, for he knew more

about barns than most of them. Sniff, sniff, sniff, he followed up to the forking-hole and stared into the black interior. There was no scent of man about the place, only the sweet scent of hay, incredible tons of hay piled up to the roof. Enough hay to feed a hundred deer for a fortnight; and there, lying contentedly on top of it, was the roe-deer they had followed.

He bade them enter, for here was warmth and food for all. He himself was as fat as butter, but they had no way of knowing that he was blind—that his eyes were sealed for all time by forest fire.

Soon the morning star would usher in another sparkling dawn, but ere night came again the wet mists would be driving in from the east.

Ten years went by. Alastaire was home on long leave to tend his property. The young laird and Callum lay below the great caldron, the Big Swamp in the distance. Both of them were using their binoculars, for it was the stalking season, and Callum muttered, "Aye, he's a muckle brute! Look at the horns of him—look at their spread! He's a sixteen-pointer, one of the old grey-faced strain, but he is going back, sir—aye, he is going back! An old hart already past his prime."

The stag was lying down just within range, a sure shot if he would rise. It was very early morning, and they could see only the horns of the great beast rising like a young oak among the scattered boulders.

"There's a hind lying behind him," Alastaire said presently. "She's dead in line—see her?"

"Yes, sir, I see her. It is yon grey-shouldered hind and—hold on now, there's another hind lying just to the right of her. We'll need to watch where we are shooting."

There was a pause, then—"It isn't a hind to the right," said Alastaire. "It's a calf. Look—he's getting up!"

As they watched, the little fellow rose, shook himself, then stretched. Somewhat sleepily he went over to where the stag was lying and stood over him. He was still in his mottled coat—a calf of last spring.

"Oh, for a camera!" sighed Alastaire. "You don't often see that, Callum, except on the picture calendars—a Royal with his favorite hind and her calf this time of the year."

"You do not," agreed Callum. "But watch your sights, sir. The calf is going to strike him up."

Alastaire glanced at his sights, and laying the

rifle down again returned to his binoculars. "I can see no other hinds—just the three of them," he said. "It's a good shot if the old chap would get up."

As he spoke the calf patted the stag on the buttocks with a slender fore-hoof, bidding him rise to the splendor of another day, but the stag did not stir. The sun had just reached them, and all round the dewdrops glistened in the heather. The calf stepped back, lowered his head, then charged full into the stag's face. It was no more than the impact of a ball of knitting-wool, and the calf fell among the old beast's legs, then scrambled up and stood staring at him defiantly.

"Oh, pretty! pretty!" muttered Alastaire. "Another greyface!"

The old stag rose idly and stooped to caress the calf's ears. They rubbed their faces together, and behind them the saddle-backed hind got up.

"Prettier still!" said Alastaire. He took up his rifle and pushed over the safety catch. He handed it to Callum, who stared at him blankly.

"Yon's an old beast, sir," he said. "It's time he was off the ground."

"I know," replied the laird. "But he's been a good stag, Callum, one of the best we ever had.

He's done a lot to establish the old greyface strain, beloved of our fathers. If you look at him now you'll see that his left ear is split."

"Well, I know it is, sir," returned Callum questioningly.

"It's Corrie of Corrie Rou, the pet of my sister's childhood," Alastaire added. "And you know it. I'm not going to shoot him, Callum. I'd rather he fell to the kindlier hand of Time."

Callum regarded his friend and master thoughtfully, then he took the rifle and removed the clip.

"Do you know, sir," said he, "it was only last year that the old woman died, she that blessed Corrie and had the second sight. She must have been the oldest soul on earth."